T0316677

In the Beyond

A Novel

Talent Madhuku

Mwanaka Media and Publishing Pvt Ltd,
Chitungwiza Zimbabwe
*
Creativity, Wisdom and Beauty

Publisher: *Mmap*
Mwanaka Media and Publishing Pvt Ltd
24 Svosve Road, Zengeza 1
Chitungwiza Zimbabwe
mwanaka@yahoo.com
mwanaka13@gmail.com
https://www.mmapublishing.org
www.africanbookscollective.com/publishers/mwanaka-media-and-publishing
https://facebook.com/MwanakaMediaAndPublishing/

Distributed in and outside N. America by African Books Collective
orders@africanbookscollective.com
www.africanbookscollective.com

ISBN: 978-1-77931-496-3
EAN: 9781779314963

© Talent Madhuku 2023

DISCLAIMER
All views expressed in this publication are those of the author and do not
necessarily reflect the views of *Mmap*.

Chapter 1

He walked at a very slow pace. As I was about to run past him, I looked at his face and he looked back at me. "Good afternoon, *Sekuru*," I greeted him, but to my surprise, he didn't respond.

He was very old, maybe in his late eighties. Deep lines of life furrowed his long and somewhat warrior like face. His bare feet, which were unusually flat, were cracked and very dirty. A single glance at him was enough to show you that he hadn't known a bath for quite some time. I was in a hurry, and I didn't want to waste my time with him, but remembering the daily counsel I always got from mother, I finally decided to greet him again.

"Good afternoon, *Sekuru*," I repeated, loudly this time.

He finally replied. "Afternoon," he said and smiled. I quickly noticed that some of his front teeth were missing.

"It's good to meet young people who still respect their elders. What name do you go by *Muzukuru?*" he asked.

"My name is Tichakunda," I said.

"That's a nice name," he said. "You know you surprised me, not many young people like to talk to old people these days, let alone a ragged old man like me."

"I am one of the few that do, *Sekuru*," I responded.

He looked ahead. "It seems we are going in the same direction," he said.

"Indeed, we are."

"Do you mind walking along with an old man?"

"Oh, not at all," I declared candidly and reduced my pace.

For a moment, we walked in silence. This allowed me to reflect on my last moments in the classroom that day, which, as usual, had not gone the way I had expected. Inside I felt a sense of guilt. I began to think of my friends whom I had left behind. During the lunch period we had agreed to take the longer route home. This route passed through an area forested by *Mutamba* trees, a favourite fruit tree of ours. With the arrival of the summer rains, the fruits were beginning to ripen and we were planning to have our first taste of this once in a year sweet-sour delicacy. Things however hadn't gone as planned. A few minutes before the first gong of the 4pm bell, our teacher had announced that we would have a spelling exercise. I thought this a bit unfair, but I hadn't been so riled up like the others. After a few missed chances, I had managed to spell a word correctly, leaving my friends who were a bit slow at spelling exercises behind.

"I think I have seen your face before. Do you live around here?" The old man finally asked, waking me from my thoughts.

"I live at Siyahokwe Secondary School. My mom teaches there," I said.

"Oh! Siyahokwe. That's a very nice school. My grandchildren go there. I attended that school too, but long back," the old man said with a warm smile. "So you are going to follow in your mother's footsteps, I hope?"

"I'm not sure; I haven't made up my mind yet. I am still deciding," I said.

"What! Why?" he exclaimed. "A lot of young boys your age already have big dreams, so what's taking you so long?"

"Well, I'll decide when I'm in high school," I replied after a moment of thought.

The old man laughed. "If I were you, I would start considering it now. In life you need to have some sort of plan, you know."

"I will think of something *Sekuru*, I definitely will," I responded although I didn't have the slightest interest in what he was saying. Being a fifth-grader at that time, I wasn't worried much about what I would do in the future. I was more concerned with the day's current events, hanging out with other kids of my age, playing hide and seek, street soccer, and other enjoyable games.

"Do you always do what you did back there? Greet people who do not respond to you?" the old man asked.

"No, l don't always do that. Why? Is it bad to greet people?" I said.

He didn't respond. He reached into one of his pockets and pulled out a cigarette. He lit it and began smoking. Is he ignoring me again? I wondered. The old man was unwell. He coughed now and again. Each cough seemed to drain something out of him. He was visibly suffering. When the coughing episodes, which always occurred after every couple of minutes ended, they left his eyes almost brimming with tears. Like we had done earlier, we walked for a while in silence. As we walked I stole a glance at the old man now and again. His sudden reticence was now making me uncomfortable. Why hadn't he responded to my question? What was he thinking? I wondered. After walking a considerable distance in silence I began thinking of increasing my pace and leaving him behind. I was about to excuse myself when the old man looked straight at me in a somewhat uneasy way.

"What's the most dangerous animal you have seen so far *Muzukuru*?" he asked.

I looked at him. "Why do you ask?" I asked.

The old man shrugged, "I'm just asking, that's all," he said.

"Well, a lion, I think it's dangerous," I replied after a moment of thought.

"Are you sure?"

"Yes, I am," I said, trying the best I could to sound confident. I had heard many stories about lions, narrations of how they sometimes escaped from game parks and attacked people. What could be more dangerous than a lion?

The old man shook his head and chuckled. He seemed extremely amused by what I had just said. "How about a gift? Have you ever received a gift?" he finally asked.

"Yes," I replied, puzzled by the nature of his questions.

"What's the most important gift you have ever received?"

I thought for a moment, "I have received many gifts from my mother and my Grandparents. All of them were important to me," I finally declared.

"But some are more important than others don't you think?" the old man remarked looking at me.

I looked down and remained silent.

"Well, I liked your responses but those aren't what I expected at all," the old man said as he glanced at the sky.

"Really?" I remarked. I was starting to feel a little annoyed. "What do you think is the most important gift then?" I inquired.

"Being able to make a choice."

"What!" I exclaimed, feeling a bit surprised by his answer.

"You heard me," the old man declared soberly.

"I am afraid I don't understand what you are saying," I said as I looked in his face. He had completely lost me.

"I didn't expect you to," the old man said, coughing. "I am old, and trust me, I have seen a lot. Experience has taught me that it's the type of choices one makes that largely determines one's destiny."

"Why are you telling me this *Sekuru*?"

The old man shrugged. "Not many young people know this, so I thought it was important that you should know."

"Oh, really? Well, so what's the most dangerous animal you have ever seen then?"

"A human being," the old man said calmly.

"What! So you mean since you are a human being yourself, you are more dangerous than a lion?" I asked sarcastically.

"You disagree?"

"Yes," I said, nodding my head. "I don't think if you were locked up in a cage with one, you'd survive."

The old man laughed, "I did not expect you to understand, nonetheless, thank you for having the patience to listen to an old man like me. I would have liked to talk to you more, but now I must take that left road. It's the one that leads where I am going," he said, looking ahead.

"That one?"

"Yes. That one," he said, nodding his head.

I waved at the old man as he went on his separate way. At that time, what he had told me didn't make sense at all so I quickly brushed the thoughts of my encounter with him aside and focused on my walk home. The road home went past a couple of bottle stores. Like any other day, men and women were sitting outside, drinking and chattering loudly among themselves. In contrast, inside one bottle store, local hit songs were being played vociferously on the radio.

Siyahokwe Secondary School, where I lived with my mother, is located in the Midlands province, in Chirumhanzu district, in the land of the Mhazi clan. It's a lovely area, with many African sugar plums, a tree that bears very delicious fruits. The year was 1992, and the month was December. A lot of folks were already looking forward to the coming year. The present one, well, it had not been that great, to say the least. The heavens had been extremely economical during the previous rain season, and most people had been left counting their losses with regards to crops and livestock. The day had been hectic. The third term was just about to end. I had done quite well that term, and I was now very much looking forward to the Christmas holiday. Having churned out heavy rains in the past few days, the skies had decided to take a break that day. But from the looks of it, it seemed as if this time around, they would be a little more generous. About to complete its quotidian journey, the sun was now just above the western horizon. It was now dusk — my best time of the day. The enigmatic cicadas, the crickets, were now concocting to reverberate their night hymns. Soon it would be dark, with a sky devoid of a single cloud to obscure the crescent moon and the countless stars.

In the distance, I could hear the cows mooing as they called their lost calves, and the shouts and whistles of cattle herders as they drove their stock home. I was now very hungry. My stomach, which hadn't given me trouble till then, started rumbling, so I increased my pace. By the time I reached home, the sun had completely set.

The teachers' place of residence was composed of fifteen houses, with a fence around it. Our house was at the far end of the compound. My mother and I had lived there ever since I could remember. As I approached home, I noticed it was unusually quiet.

From a long way off, I could hear dogs barking. A startled rat dashed in front of me, its nimble steps bearing crackling sounds on the fallen dry guava leaves scattered in front of the house. Inside, the lights had not yet been switched on. Was mum still at work? I wondered. I looked for the keys under the rug, where we usually hid them, but I couldn't find them. I tried to open the door and was surprised to find it unlocked. I went in, turned on the light and rushed straight to get some food. The kitchen door was wide open, so I walked in, only to freeze after a few steps. I couldn't believe what I was seeing. All the strength in my body left me. Mother was lying motionless on the floor with a kitchen knife buried deep in her chest.

Chapter 2

Eva stood in front of her house, contemplating while gazing at her flowers. She loved flowers and had a variety of them in her yard. Eva was especially fond of the lotus flower, which she viewed as a symbol of beauty, fertility and wealth. Also fascinated by Arums, she had lots of them in her yard, and they constituted the bulk of her flowers. The flowers lifted her spirits every time she ventured into her garden. Today was different though. Being exactly two years since her husband had passed away, she was feeling sad. Gazing at her surroundings: her house, the lone Jacaranda tree in the yard and then back at the flowers, she sighed. It was like something was missing. She was beginning to grow discontent with the ambience. With her son growing a little detached, she felt as if her life had entered a period of endless forlornness.

Today, not even the Arums, with their unadulterated white flower spathes and their beautiful lush green leaves, could lift her depressed soul. It seemed today was going to be one of those bad days. Eva felt as if she was being suffocated. She had begun having these episodes when her husband died and it seemed they were becoming worse and more frequent as the days went by. After standing for a while, staring blankly at her flowers, her legs began complaining and she slowly dragged herself to a bench in front of her house and sat down. What was she going to do today? How was she going to spend her day? She wondered. She knew she needed something to distract her from the sad thoughts she was having. Maybe a visit to her family business would help, she decided. The family business, Kam Enterprises, was an electronics shop which she jointly managed with her son. Her father-in-law had started the business, and after his death, his only son, Eva's husband, had taken up the reins of the business. Now that he was also gone, the button had been left with her and her son. The thought of her son sent a chill down Eva's spine. Her son had grown a little distant lately. Why? She couldn't figure it out. She loved her son so much and his sudden reserve was hurting her so deeply. She yearned for the close bond she used to have with him. She missed those times when he'd come to her, sometimes crying, to confer with her when something troubled him. Eva sighed.

Things had changed. Her son now kept everything to himself.

Tired of pondering and sitting alone in her garden, Eva finally got up and went into the house. She was busy going through her clothes, looking for one of her dresses when she heard the sound of an approaching car. She peeped through the window to check who it was and saw her friend, Tanya, parking in her driveway. Eva immediately beamed and rushed outside. It had been a while since her friend had visited. When Tanya disembarked from her car, they embraced and went into the house.

"Can I make you some tea?" Eva asked when they had comfortably settled in the living room.

Tanya smiled, "Do you still have that herb tea?"

Eva nodded. "I still have some."

"Please, that would be nice."

"Okay then," Eva said and went into her kitchen. Tanya followed her.

"So what have you been up to lately?" Eva asked.

Tanya shrugged, "you know, the same thing I always do, work," she said as she looked around, admiring the tableware in the kitchen. As she walked around the kitchen, a set of tea mugs finally caught her attention. "These tea mugs, where did you get them?" she said and picked one.

"I bought them in town," Eva responded casually, carefully handling the kettle from the stove.

"You should show me the place. I need a set of tea mugs just like this for my kitchen," Tanya said.

"Don't worry," Eva said, pouring tea into a tea cup and handing it to her friend. "The next time we go into town, I will show you the place."

"So where is Dean? Is he around?" Tanya asked.

"He's not here," Eva said, shaking her head, "maybe he is at the shop, maybe not, I don't know. These past months, something has been happening to my son. He's grown a little distant," she said in a rather sad manner.

"Come on, Eva. You can't expect him to behave like he did when he was still a young boy. Can't you see that he is all grown up now?" Tanya said.

"I know girl, but trust me, there is something wrong. He is too reserved these days, and the crowd he's been hanging around these past months look suspicious."

"He drove by my house yesterday," Tanya said.

Eva put her cup down and looked at her friend.

"He did," Tanya said. "And the day before yesterday when I was driving home I saw him parked near that big pine in my street and when he saw me he quickly drove away."

"Are you sure it was him?"

"Yes. I am absolutely sure."

"You don't think…"

"Oh I know something is going on. Susan has been behaving strangely these past few days."

Eva remained quiet and sipped her tea. Was this the reason why her friend had visited? She wondered. She raised her head and looked at her friend. Looking at Tanya always brought back memories of her childhood. How fast time had moved. It seemed like yesterday when she and Tanya skipped the rope in front of her father's house. Those were happy times. They were young, innocent and did almost everything together. Over the years many things had happened between them; they had disagreed on many things, they had fought countless times but ultimately, they had managed to remain friends. However, because of this new development, Eva wondered if things were going to remain that way. Her friend had two beautiful daughters, the older one Susan, worked as a pharmacist, and the younger one, Anika, was still in college. Eva knew her friend well. If there was anything Tanya treasured, it was her two daughters.

"Do you want me to do anything Tanya?" Eva finally said to her friend.

Tanya shrugged. "No," she said

"Why?" Eva asked.

"They are adults Eva. And even if we intervene, you think they will stop? Let's let them be. Besides, I am tired Eva, I am tired of always fighting with my daughter. If I am to be honest with you, after the boys I have seen her with, trust me, your son will be a huge improvement for her."

"How long has this been going on?" Eva asked.

"I don't know, probably for a while. I was preoccupied with work to notice."

Eva thought for a moment. "Well, I know you said we should do nothing but I think I will have a chat with my son." she said. "He's a bit of a player and I think you know that. If I just sit around and do nothing this might end up costing us dearly."

"They won't like it," Tanya said looking worried.

"It doesn't matter," Eva said. "We are their mothers. We suffered the agonies of child birth in order to bring them into this world. If we give them advice it's not because we want to control them, it's because we care."

"Well, I will have a chat with my daughter too then." Tanya said. She seemed deep in thought. She sipped her tea and looked outside through the kitchen window. "So how is your friend?" she finally asked.

"Who?"

"Come on. You know who I am talking about," Tanya giggled and leaned towards the direction of Eva's neighbour.

"I don't know. Why do you even ask? You know too well that I don't talk to her," Eva said, looking disgusted.

"Well, I thought you guys had reconciled."

"Come on! Reconciled? Really? She is pregnant again, by the way."

"What!" Tanya exclaimed.

"She is," Eva said, now laughing.

"Again? For goodness sake, how many does she want to have?"

"Who knows," Eva said, still laughing.

Tanya shook her head, "that woman is something else," she said. She stood up and picked up her purse, "Girl, I need to get going."

"So soon?" Eva asked.

"I could have stayed longer but there are some things that I need to attend to," Tanya said. "Don't forget to show me where you got those beautiful mugs."

"I won't forget," Eva said, accompanying Tanya out to her car. After her friend had left, Eva went back into her house and washed the tea cups they had used. Her friend's visit had cheered her up. She was now feeling much better. She cancelled her planned visit to the shop and began preparing her lunch. What her friend had said, was it true? How would her son react if she confronted him? Wouldn't he become angry with her? She wondered. She was wary of her son. She had seen him hurt a lot of young women before and she hoped his intentions were sincere this time. After she'd finished her lunch, she went into her late husband's study to look for a book to read. Eva was a voracious reader. She liked reading. For her, reading was like therapy. It healed her soul. After walking back and forth, going through the book shelves she finally picked one. It was a small volume she had never seen before. *Notes from the underground*: the title read.

Chapter 3

"Ticha! Tichakunda. Wake up!" I heard a languid voice calling me as if from a long-distance away. Sometimes, when something bad happens, something really bad, everything, on the face of it, ceases to exist, and all that is seemingly left, would be the mental picture of that traumatic event. As I lay sprawled on the cold floor without any comprehension of where I was, the horrifying image of my mother laying in a pool of blood, vivid and so real as if I was actually still standing and looking at her, kept forcing itself into my mind, over and over again.

"Tichakunda!" I heard the voice again, louder this time. At this moment I could not clearly see the person who was calling me. It was still an obscure moment for me. My body ached. I've felt lots of pain over the years, but nothing comes close to what I felt as I lay on that cold floor.

"Tichakunda!" The voice called again. I heard it more clearly this time and instantly recognised it. It was Mrs Mumba's voice. Mrs Mumba lived in the house opposite to ours and was very close to my mother.

"Tichakunda!" she said again, picking me from where I was lying. She carried me to the living room where she laid me on the sofa

"Tichakunda! Look at me," she said, shaking me gently, "hey boy! Look at me. What happened?"

"I want to talk to my mum. I think she is hurt. I want to see her." I said. Tears were now coming out of my eyes; I couldn't stop them. I just couldn't. Mrs Mumba looked at me and paused for a moment. "You will see her," she eventually said, "for the moment, why don't we go to my house first?" she said, lifting me without even waiting for my response. Being a very ample woman, she didn't even give me the time to react. She quickly took me to her house before I could resist.

When we entered the house, we were greeted by Mr Mumba, who was seated on his sofa watching the 6 pm news.

"Is something wrong?" he asked his wife after noticing how she was carrying me.

Mrs Mumba placed me on the sofa. "Stay here, my boy. It's going to be okay," she reassured.

Mr Mumba briefly looked at me and then immediately turned to his wife. "Is everything okay?" he asked again.

"Can we talk outside, please?" Mrs Mumba replied, beckoning her husband to go outside.

Once they were outside, I heard Mrs Mumba and her husband whispering, and then all of a sudden, I heard loud footsteps of someone running outside towards our house.

"Hey! Chisvo!" Mr Mumba shouted, "stop and come back here."

"Where is she?" I heard Chisvo asking.

"Do you know what I don't like, Chisvo?" Mr Mumba replied sternly, "what I don't like is to repeat myself."

I decided to go outside to see for myself what was happening. As I stepped outside, I saw Chisvo walking towards the Mumbas.

"You don't understand, it's my wife, I have just found out that she came here, and I have every reason to believe she might have done something terrible," Chisvo said, his voice cracking.

"Oh really?" Mr Mumba remarked, his voice heavily loaded with sarcasm, "you know what, you just came at the right time. I was about to call the police, so don't worry, you can tell them that story of yours when they arrive."

I always try to avoid thinking of my mother. I do this not because I don't want to remember her. I do this because every time I think of her, the image of her lying in a pool of blood, with a knife buried deep in her chest, is the first one that floods my mind. It pains me that this should happen because I have many beautiful memories of her. For some unknown reason, they have receded into the deepest realm of my mind and I always have to strain myself in order to reach them. It takes me sometime to draw them back, but when I do, it's as if she is standing right in front of me again. I can see the warm smile she gave me when I arrived home early from school, the perfect lines that formed on her face every time she read to me from some of her favourite books. At first though the memories are rather hazy, like the early hours of a foggy morning. But just as the fog disappears with the rise of the sun, when I exert myself long enough, the memories also become clearer with the passing of time.

My mother didn't like to talk to me about her past. As a result, much of what I know about her childhood is what my Grandmother told me. My mother was the youngest of three siblings, who included her sister Chipo and her brother, Mandikomborera. Of the three, she was the only one who had completed her studies. The other two had dropped out midway through their secondary education. Although my mother had a close relationship with her brother, her relationship with her sister was strained.

When she finished her secondary studies, my mother enrolled into a teacher's college, where she became close friends with one of her colleagues. He was an orphan who had managed to pursue his education through scholarships. Just after my mother had fallen pregnant with me, he had a tragic accident that claimed his life. This seemed to have heartbroken my mother because, growing up, I rarely saw men around her. She was a very independent woman. Things however changed in the third term of my fifth grade, when a new teacher by the name of Chisvo began teaching at the school. He was fairly young, probably the same age as my mother, and like her, he taught English.

A few days after his arrival, he and mum became the best of friends. Chisvo began frequenting our home, bringing books with him which he read and discussed with mum.

Unaccustomed to having a man around my mother, I didn't like this new development at all and I avoided Chisvo the best I could whenever he visited. Chisvo must have realised my slight resentment because he tried his best to befriend me. He would bring me something whenever he visited, and he somehow knew all my favourite snacks— those potato chips I liked so much, sweet biscuits and chocolate candy, yet despite all of this, I couldn't find it in my heart to like him.

Though I was still quite young, I was pretty suspicious that there was much more between him and my mother than just friendship. It didn't take long for my suspicions to be confirmed.

One weekend, I overheard my mother and Mrs Mumba talking.

"Are you sure you are not rushing into this?" Mrs Mumba asked.

"I am just getting to know him better. He seems honest to me."

"Come on, don't they all portray themselves as such?" Mrs Mumba said and laughed.

"They do but I think I ought to give this one a try. I have to, it has taken me a long time to let someone into my life once again," Mum replied.

"I do understand what you are saying, but I think you should do a little digging. Do you know that my husband has two other children with two different women, and he hid this only for me to find out later when we were already married?"

"Really! How did you find out?" Mother asked, seemingly surprised.

"One of the kids wanted a birth certificate, and the child's mother came to my house looking for him. That's how I found out."

"Oh! That must have been very upsetting."

"Upsetting? Girl, I was devastated," Mrs Mumba said. "Those kids have to go to school, and they need food and other necessities as well. My husband is the one who has to take care of all that, and this leaves our budget strained since I don't work. I am actually considering going back to school through correspondence."

"You should do that," mother said. "And if you want my help, don't be afraid to ask. I didn't know that you were going through something like this,"

"Well, now you know. That's why you need to be careful," Mrs Mumba said, her voice exhibiting shades of sadness.

I have always asked myself how things would have turned out if my mother had seriously heeded Mrs Mumba's advice. How our lives could have turned out, but it doesn't matter now. A few weeks later, after that conversation with Mrs Mumba, I found myself sitting with my Grandparents at her funeral. This was my first time at a burial, and it turned out to be the burial of the most important person in my life. The whole event was just so lamentable. It's one of those sad experiences I wish I could forget, yet no matter how I try, I still can't get it out of my mind. I still vividly remember every moment of it, like it was yesterday. I can still hear the crying women. All the songs hummed by the aged women sitting around her body the night before the burial, songs so deep and melancholy that they bring tears to my eyes.

It had been established, after some investigations, that Chisvo's wife had stabbed my mother. She had caught wind of the affair from blabbers within the school cottages just after her arrival from Chisvo's rural home, where she lived. My mother was Ndau, and according to their culture, her death was viewed as a bad death since she'd been murdered. After learning of what had happened, my Grandparents had not been amused at all and had vowed to seek retribution for their daughter's death. The Ndau are regarded as very spiritual people skilled in the art of herbalism and black magic. Because of this reputation, Chisvo's relatives and in-laws were greatly unsettled by my Grandparents' utterances and before my mother's burial, their emissaries visited my Grandparents and agreed to pay some cattle. This was done to appease the spirit of the deceased, I was told.

My Grandparents lived in Chikore, an area within Chipinge district. It's a land with fertile soils and an equable climate. The famous Chirinda forest, which is home to the renowned Big Tree, is not that far away.

After the funeral, I found solace in the company of my Uncle, Mandikomborera, who stayed with us for a week. He told me many fascinating stories about Harare, where he was based.

"Hey nephew," he called me one day, "would you like to go fishing with me?"

"Yes Uncle. I would like that a lot, but I have never gone fishing before," I replied.

"Don't worry," Uncle smiled. "I'll teach you," he said and gently patted my shoulder.

The next morning, after we had finished our breakfast, he took me to the Nyagadza River. This river flowed all year round and was a lifeline to the people of Chikore. As we walked to the river, Uncle Mandi told me that the river had a lot of catfish and river bream, and he and his friends used to catch a lot of fish back in his teenage years. I gladly listened to what he said and looked around. Chikore looked beautiful in summer. Bathed by the heavy summer rains, the surrounding grass, trees and shrubs looked crispy green. A light breeze blew now and again, producing a low soothing rustle. Many flying insects buzzed around; colourful butterflies, bees, flying beetles, and on the ground, termites and ants had already emerged.

"I love this pool, I call it *Muzi*," Uncle said when we reached a large pool that was adjacent to some rapids.

"Why do you call it by that name?" I asked.

"It's my safe haven, one of the few places around here where I can unwind without being bothered," he said as he placed his fishing lines and the container that contained the bait on the ground. He then proceeded to pick a giant worm from the bait container. I watched with great interest as he attached the worm to the hook.

"There," he exclaimed. "Try that on this one," he said, handing me another fishing rod. I picked a worm and tried to attach it on the hook. After a couple of attempts, Uncle Mandi finally nodded his head in approval.

"Impeccable, that will do," he said with a smile.

We sat silently on a spot which he'd indicated as great for catching the fish. "Why do we have to be so quiet?" I whispered after a while.

"If we make a lot of noise, we'll scare away the fish," he replied in a low voice.

The day proceeded well. The whole activity proved to be very serene and yet interesting. Now and again, I found myself being drawn to the sounds of the birds — the magnificent chirrup notes of sparrows, loud songs of the beautiful black headed orioles. A mourning dove would call nearby, and to my intense delight, once in a while, a fish would swim to the surface of the pool, creating a beautiful circular ripple. Uncle Mandi caught a reasonable amount of river bream, one medium-sized catfish, and he was delighted with his efforts. As for me, well, I didn't catch anything.

"Don't worry, nephew. You will get them next time," he said and patted me on my shoulder.

As we walked back home, I asked him about the city where he lived. He told me that he owned a small store in a place called Mbare. This place was the biggest bus terminus which linked the capital city to other major towns. His face beamed when he talked about his small business. He was very fond of it, I could tell. Things were going quite well, he said. He had raised more capital and he was planning to open another small shop in a different location within the city.

"You know, nephew, one of these coming holidays, I'm going to take you with me to the city," he said, days later, before he left. "Would you like that?"

"I would," I beamed.

"Good, it's settled then," he said.

After Uncle left, I spent the following days with my Grandparents preparing for my new school. I was also able to visit the new school before the opening day. Rebai Primary was about two miles away, which was much closer than my previous school.

As we approached the beginning of the new term, Grandma bought me a new uniform and some new stationery. "Hey, Tichakunda, come here," she called me immediately after returning from the shops where she had bought the items. "I got you a new uniform," she said when I entered the kitchen hut where she was sitting. "Try it on. I want to see if it fits."

I took the uniform to my room. It emitted a pleasant odour. I liked it. When I finished putting it on, I immediately ran back to the kitchen to show Grandma. "There, I knew it would fit you, my grandson," she exclaimed when I came back to the hut.

"Thank you so much, Grandma."

"Don't even mention it, grandson," she said, "I want you to go to that school and beat those other kids like your mum used to do."

"I'll try my best Grandma," I replied.

"I know you will, dear; I know you will," she smiled. "Now remove that uniform and come back for breakfast. Call your Grandpa for me, tell him breakfast is ready."

Grandma served breakfast, tea and a starchy tuber which looked like sweet potatoes. After taking my first bite, I made a face.

"What's wrong, grandson?" Grandfather asked, laughing. "Haven't you eaten cassava before?"

"Well, this is my first time eating it, but it's okay Grandpa," I said.

"My dear grandson, you are not very good at lying, are you?" Grandma remarked. "There's some rice I left last night in that blue basin which is on top of the cupboard. You can have it if you like," she said. I gratefully stood up from where I was sitting and took the basin. I liked rice; I liked it better.

"He surely is growing up quickly, isn't he?" Grandma said, looking at Grandfather.

"He is," Grandpa nodded in agreement, his mouth still full of cassava. "He is," he said.

Chapter 4

The time was approaching noon when Kam arrived at the flats. Ignoring John, who was gesturing him to come closer, he parked his car a few metres from the housing block and casually stepped out. So these were the flats he had heard so much about? He thought as he looked around. He did not like what he saw at all. The flats were in a deplorable condition. Piles and piles of plastics, bottles, used pampers and other uncollected trash lay everywhere.

"I thought with all that money you have been getting, you would be living in a much better place," he remarked dryly.

John shrugged, "I like it here."

"Can we go inside? We need to talk?" Kam said, looking at the barefooted children playing with a tattered plastic ball a few metres from where they were standing.

John stiffened. "I wouldn't recommend that boss," he said. "I haven't cleaned my room yet. It's a mess."

"It doesn't matter," Kam said. "I am not much of an orderly person myself."

"Okay," John said. "Let's go inside."

Many of the building's tenants were out and about, and most of the doors they passed on their way to John's room were closed. However, in the few slightly open ones which Kam managed to peep through as they walked past, he was surprised to see entire families of five people and sometimes even more, crammed inside.

"They all live here together?" he asked John as they walked past.

"Yes they do," John said casually.

John's room was on the third floor of the building. When they reached it John had to wrestle with the lock for a while before they could get in. He hadn't exaggerated at all when he said the room was a mess. Kam had to struggle to keep a straight face when he walked inside. The room smelled of sweat and burnt-up food. Soiled clothes were scattered everywhere. The floor, which Kam could tell had not been swept for days, was littered with crumbs of food and pieces of cigarette stubs.

"Have a seat," John offered Kam a chair, the only one in the room. "You said you had something important you wanted to discuss, boss?"

Kam decided to get straight to the point. "I am here about those missing drugs, John," he said

"The missing drugs? I thought we settled that issue days ago."

"They know John," Kam said.

"What are you talking about, boss?"

"They know you took the drugs. Delight and his people will come for you if you do not return those drugs."

"But I didn't take the drugs, boss," John said. He seemed completely unflustered by what Kam had just said.

"John, don't do this. We can still salvage this situation. Just give me the drugs and all will be forgiven," Kam said. He thought if he pleaded with him, John would break down and confess but that's not what happened.

"I didn't take the drugs, boss," John insisted.

Kam suddenly felt a surge of anger enveloping him. "I know you took them John and I have proof," he said.

John remained silent. He seemed to be waiting for something, possibly for Kam to show him the proof.

Kam became frustrated. Why was John doing this? Didn't John see he was here to help? Kam wondered. Unable to contain his anger anymore, Kam stood up and left the room. John closely followed behind him. *You traitor!* Kam thought, burning inside with anger. Outside, the group of adolescence who were playing soccer briefly stopped what they were doing and stared at him. John waved at them, "they are surprised to see you here. Few men of your calibre come here, you know."

Kam didn't respond to this. He entered his car, and stared hard at John before he drove off. He was now feeling a bit stiff, desperately in need of something to calm his nerves. He drove his Toyota Camry along Harare road and turned into 16th Street, where he stopped at a bar. There, he bought a lager and a packet of cigarettes. The little bar had two barmaids, and one of them, the one who served him, immediately caught his eye. She was about his height, dark in complexion, with a small mole just above her left eye. As she was serving him his beer Kam winked at her and to his immense pleasure she winked back at him. Sensing he might have a chance with her, Kam remained at the counter and watched her work. It was fun to watch her work. Her tight fitting dress and her graceful movements mesmerised him. After watching her work for almost half an hour he finally decided to approach her. He half expected her to get angry but she did not. She just looked at him and giggled. That's a good sign, he thought and kept looking at her.

The bar maid continued her tasks, smiling shyly when she looked up and realised he was still gazing at her. A few minutes later, looking at him, she finally left the counter and walked out of the small bar. Kam checked to see if no one had noticed and then drawing his wallet from his pocket, he followed her with a big grin.

An hour later, Kam was back in his shop. His shop, found along Leopold Takawira Street, in the city centre, offered electrical appliances which he imported mainly from Japan and China. When he was at the shop, Kam usually spent most of his time in the small office located at the rear. This is where he managed the shop's books and where he received friends and business colleagues whenever they came to visit. As he sat in his chair, staring at his father's framed picture on the wall, Kam began to think of the years gone by. He recalled how visiting the small office used to bring him untold joy, how his father greeted him with a warm smile whenever he visited. Those were happy times. Thanks to his father, the shop's retail operations ran smoothly back then. Whatever the changing business environment threw at him, his father, who undoubtedly possessed a knack for business, always managed to weather the storm.

When his father passed away, leaving him and his mother, Kam never imagined that he would run into any major problems. He thought his father had taught him everything he needed to know. Though he had this self-confidence, things immediately went off course when he took over the business. His mother, who hadn't involved herself with the business when his father was still alive, leaving everything in his father's hands, watched as he struggled to keep it afloat. After seeing him struggle for a whole year, she could not take it any longer. She stopped behaving as a silent partner and began to help with the day to day management of the business. When she came in, she proposed a scheme in which the shop would offer electric appliances to civil servants on credit. The targeted customers would be required to pay monthly instalments until they settled their accounts. A few months after adopting the credit scheme, sales gradually picked up again. Stock which used to take almost half a year to clear out now barely lasted a month. Kam and his mother were over the moon because of this success. Their happiness did not last though, as the days went by, they realised that their operating costs had also increased. In an effort to solve this issue, they began discussing the possibility of importing their merchandise through the Port of Beira. They also contemplated starting a new business in Mozambique. The country was just coming out of a lengthy civil war, and they hoped to exploit any new business opportunities that could arise with the ushering in of a new peaceful era. After some consultations with business colleagues and other professionals who had a deeper knowledge of the country, they decided to import a consignment of goods through the port of Beira.

Toward the end of 1992, Kam travelled to Mozambique to receive the shipment. When he arrived in the port city of Beira, he discovered that the goods had not yet arrived, so to pass time, he decided to roam around the town as he waited for the shipment to arrive. As he roamed around he noticed with distress that the lengthy civil war had taken its toll on the town. Most of the infrastructure had been badly damaged. In some sections, burnt-out cars, rocks and concrete rubble still blocked the streets. The town was still in distress, the lacerations caused by the war, clearly visible and fresh, needed more time for them to fully heal.

After almost an hour of roaming around, Kam noticed a small bar that was open and approached it. On the veranda stood a teenager who was holding a bundle of newspapers.

Kam bought one and walked in. There weren't many people inside the small bar. Beside the bartender, Kam only saw three people; two young fellows chatting in a language he did not understand, and a visibly drunk elderly gentleman who was seated near the counter.

Taking care not to engage in conversation with any of the three men, Kam bought a beer and retired to one of the three small tables in the bar where he began to read his paper. Many of the stories inside were about peace and reconciliation. The local officials were promising the local people and international Investors stability after the lengthy and devastating civil war. In international news there was a story about a report which had been recently released by the World Meteorological Organisation. The report detailed an unprecedented level of ozone depletion in both the Arctic and Antarctic. Kam skimmed through the story on the WMO's report and then went to the sports section where he began to read a short bio of the US Open champion, Stefan Edberg. He was about to finish reading the article when a man who seemed to be in love with his beard entered the bar. After buying a beer at the counter, the man waved at him. Kam smiled and waved back. Taking this as an allurement for dialogue, the man walked from where he was standing and came to Kam's table.

"Is there anything interesting in there?" he said.

"Interesting?"

"I meant in the paper," the man said. "Anyway, it was a stupid thing to ask. May I?" he signalled if he could sit.

"Yes, no problem," Kam replied.

"This is a nice place."

"It is," Kam agreed. He liked the interior of the small bar, it was well lit and warm. In contrast to what he had felt when he walked outside, Kam felt he could relax once again. He also liked the colour used on the walls. Showing all signs of having been recently repainted, the interior walls sported one of his favourite colours; a radiant shade of light green.

"So are you one of the locals or you are passing through?" the man asked as he picked some pages of the newspaper which Kam was still to read from the table.

"I am here on business," Kam replied.

"What sector?"

"Retail. I sell electronic appliances."

"Is the business good? Are you making money?"

"Well, there have been some ups and downs, but I can't complain," Kam replied.

"That's good, I am in business myself?" the man said.

Kam smiled. "I suspected you might. What kind of business are you involved in?"

The man regarded Kam for a moment and then drew a tiny sachet from his pocket and handed it to Kam.

Kam inspected the sachet for a moment and then handed it back.

"Nice aroma. Where do you get it from?" he asked.

"I have connections here," the man said and took a sip of his beer. His name was Delight. He was based in SA but he regularly came to Mozambique to monitor his business operations. The conflict had made it easier for him to conduct his business. He had dependable connections here and he was now making a lot of money. Kam listened patiently to the man but found it hard to believe half of what he said.

"So you are telling me you make a lot of money doing this kind of thing?" he asked.

Delight regarded him for a moment and then stood up. "Come with me. I want to show you something," he said. Kam picked up his beer and followed his intriguing companion outside.

"What do you think?" Delight said, pointing at a new 1989 Mercedes Benz 560sl vehicle.

Kam could hardly hide his surprise. "It's yours?"

"Of course it's mine," Delight said.

"And you get all this from selling weed?" Kam asked in disbelief.

"Well, I also deal in rare merchandise," Delight said casually.

"Rare merchandise?"

"Yes, things like rare animal hides and tusks. These goods are highly sought after in certain circles and whenever my clients want them, I procure."

"I imagine you make a lot of money by doing this," Kam remarked.

Delight shrugged. "Not much, my cash cow is weed. There is a high demand for it. You look like a very smart business man, you should join the fold. As a matter of fact, I want to offer you a deal which I think you might be interested in."

"What kind of deal?"

Delight reached into his pockets and pulled out a packet of cigarettes. "It's simple. I want you to transport a few kilos of my stuff across the border and deliver them to a certain someone. You will get 20 percent of the profit for your troubles."

Kam took a sip of his beer, "no offence, my friend, but I think I'll pass."

"Come on, seriously? I thought you would be more open-minded than this," Delight said.

"I'm sorry. Drugs are not my thing. Besides, what do you think will happen if I get caught?"

"You won't," Delight said.

Kam remained silent and looked towards the direction of the harbour.

"I do understand your fears, but trust me, my friend, the risks are very low. How about I increase your share of profits to 40 percent?" Delight proposed.

"40 percent? How much is that?"

"A lot trust me."

"I don't know," Kam said, "I am just not sure about this."

Delight smiled. He was sensing a breakthrough, "you'll never regret this, trust me. I am friends with the people at the border, they won't give you any trouble."

Kam did not say anything. He remained quiet, thinking. If he agreed to this deal, would he get into trouble, would he get caught? He wondered. Despite knowing the high risk involved, he eventually agreed to the deal. Like he had been promised, he did not encounter any problems at the border or at any point along the way. When he arrived in Harare, he quickly dropped the package at the agreed meeting point with Delight's man.

The man, who introduced himself as Maromo, advised Kam that his share of the profits would be brought to him at his shop. Kam readily agreed to the arrangement, he was more than happy to have the bags of weed off his hands. A week passed, and another one. On the fourth day of the third week, when Kam was starting to have doubts about the whole thing, Maromo finally arrived at the shop. Kam invited the fellow into his office, and after exchanging a few pleasantries, Maromo reached into his bag and pulled out a huge bundle of twenty-dollar notes.

"Is this all mine?" Kam asked.

Maromo smiled and stood up to leave. "Of course, it's all yours. If you still want to work with us, Mr Delight will be very much interested in talking to you," he said, handing Kam a note with Delight's number on it.

The bundle of notes amounted to a thousand dollars. Kam was astounded. So there was a lot of money in this kind of business after all. He thought as he stared at the notes lying on his table. Just how much money would he make if he joined the weed business? He wondered. He spend the rest of the day weighing pros and cons of joining but his mind was already made up. The amount of money that could be made was just too much for him to resist. In the ensuing months Kam made several trips to Mozambique to collect the product. It wasn't difficult for him to bring in the product because of Delight's connections at the border. He made a killing during this time. He even started another retail business in Mutare, which he managed independently to hide his activities from his mother. After a year or so of doing business with Delight, the drug kingpin advised him that it would be okay if he also sold his own weed on the side. Kam was overjoyed, only to realise that finding the right people who could sell his product on the ground wasn't easy at all. Having only concentrated on getting the drugs safely across the border, while Delight's people did the rest of the job on the ground, he hadn't appreciated how difficult it was to sell the product to the consumers.

After days of thinking on the subject, in which he briefly considered taking on one of his shop employees, he finally decided to recruit John, his family's housekeeper. He trusted John, and because of his history with him, he knew they could work well together. It took time to convince John. However, as Kam expected,

John proved to be a valuable recruit when he finally relented. He knew the streets and he was loyal. Kam was very pleased with his performance, and as the months passed, he gradually began to depend on him.

Recent events, however, had completely left Kam baffled and bitter. Just a month ago, a break-in had occurred at their stash house in Mbare and about forty kilos of weed had been taken. A few weeks after the stash house break in, Maromo, Delight's main man on the streets, noticed a sudden increase in John's spending. Intrigued by this sudden change in John's fortune, he began monitoring him. It took Maromo only a few days to confirm his suspicions. John was privately selling the stolen drugs on the side.

Chapter 5

The remainder of the holiday went by quite quickly for me. It was also a busy one. People were still hustling with planting their crops. Many chores needed to be done, so Grandpa decided to employ an extra pair of hands to help around the homestead. He hired Danda, a man who proved to be very helpful, especially with taking care of the cattle, which had lately been giving us trouble by invading people's fields.

A day before the opening day of school, I felt bored of always being at home and decided to explore the area around my Grandparents' homestead. There is a hill nearby. Woody, with a lot of giant granite boulders, it was my obvious choice. I didn't have much difficult climbing up the hill. When I reached the top, I searched and found a comfortable rock on which I sat. The view was quite exceptional. From where I was sitting, I saw my new school, the local growth point, and a carpet of healthy crops in the fields. After a while though, I became bored again and decided to visit the pool where I had gone fishing with my Uncle.

Strolling casually, I hummed softly as I went on my way, picking wild berries, which I gladly enjoyed. As I was about to reach the pool, I heard moaning sounds coming from the nearby bushes. Struck by a bolt of curiosity, I stopped to listen. Who could it be who was behind the bushes? And what could they possibly be doing to make such a peculiar noise? I wondered. I crouched and silently began to move slowly towards the sounds until I could make out two figures in an opening behind the bushes. Buck naked, the two were utterly immersed in a world of their own. One was a young girl who wasn't much older than I was, maybe fourteen or a little older. The other was a young man who I could tell was in his early twenties. Fearing that if I stayed longer, I might be discovered, I didn't stick around. I left the spot as quietly as I had arrived and proceeded to the pool. The pool was still as beautiful as it had been the very first time I had seen it. Due to its unadulterated state, I concluded that possibly very few cattle, if any, came to drink at the pool. There was this shallow spot at the edge where you could see the sparkling sand particles below. I approached it, removed my shoes and waded in. The water was cool, with a soothing effect to it. About a metre or so from where I stood, water scavenger beetles whirled impressively on the water surface, their smooth, oval, black bodies shining brilliantly in the summer sunlight. I moved towards them, thinking I could catch one, but they quickly dashed away.

The peaceful moment didn't last long though, just after a couple of minutes or so, I heard some footsteps behind me. I turned round to look and found myself facing the girl I had just seen before. She froze when she saw me. She was now alone, and from the way she was acting, I could tell she had not expected to see anyone at the pool. With hesitation, she approached me.

"Hi," she said.

"Hi," I replied, not quite sure what to make of the current awkward situation.

"I haven't seen your face before. Are you new here?" she asked shyly.

"Yes, I am," I said.

I wasn't feeling comfortable talking to the girl. I got out of the pool, picked up my shoes and started leaving.

"Hey, wait, what's your name?" the girl asked.

I hesitated, "I am Tichakunda," I finally said.

"I am Shorai," she said. "Where do you live?"

"I live with the Bungiras. I am their grandson."

The girl smiled, "we are neighbours. It's funny that we haven't met before," she said. "Would you mind waiting for me while I wash my feet so we can walk back home together?" she asked, looking straight at me.

I remained quiet for a while, thinking about the awkwardness of walking home with her. I wasn't comfortable walking with her after what I had seen her doing, however, I eventually agreed to wait because I didn't want to be seen as discourteous. As we walked home she told me about her life. She had done well in her grade seven exams. She was about to begin her first year of secondary education and was very much looking forward to it, she said. I listened quietly as she chatted incessantly, wondering what she would do if I told her that I had actually seen her prior to our meeting at the river that day, but I decided against it.

When I reached home, I went straight to my hut and checked if all my school items were in order. I put all my exercise books in my small satchel, polished my school shoes and then sat on my bed reading a novel called *The Treasure Island*, which I found very exciting. Later, I went to the kitchen for the evening supper. I didn't stay long in the kitchen that night. Immediately after finishing my meal, I wished my Grandparents a good night and went to bed.

My first day at the new school went very well. In class, we sat according to our grades in rows and on tables of four. I was told that this was done to help teachers quickly identify students that required special assistance in their studies. Due to this arrangement, I was assigned to a table at the back of the class. I had failed to produce my academic report, which had been misplaced during the chaotic period before my mother's burial. Three other kids shared my table. Two were girls.

"Hello," the third member of the table, Peter, greeted me when I first sat at the table, to which the two girls laughed. People called him Blackface. He was very dark and stout.

"Hi," I replied, "how are you?"

"I am fine," he said. The two girls, Ruramai and Jane, continued their annoying giggling, which, I realised, was directed at Peter.

I looked at them and frowned, "what's so funny?" I asked. They did not respond. They just looked down and remained quiet.

"It is okay, don't mind them," Peter said, looking directly at me.

"Are you sure?" I asked him.

"Yes, they do that all the time," Peter said, seemingly not perturbed by the whole situation. He was a funny character, and from that day, I could not help but admire how he handled all the awkward situations that he faced in his everyday life because of his looks. A non-member of the hygiene department, most girls at school, poked fun at him. Peter never reacted to their teases, though. He just remained quiet and went about his business. You could always get away with the teasing if you were a girl, though. If you happened to be a boy, well, things could get ugly.

"Hey Blackface," a seventh grade called him one day. "What did you eat yesterday? Did you eat a skunk or something?"

Peter froze in his tracks, turned and faced the boy. "What did you say to me?" he asked with a very calm voice.

"You heard what I said."

Peter drew closer to the boy and patted him lightly on the shoulder. "Listen, my friend, and listen very carefully. If you ever say something like that to me again, I will remove each and every tooth in your mouth. Do you feel me?"

"What!" the boy exclaimed and started laughing loudly. I couldn't blame him. At that time, what Peter had said seemed funny. There was no way under the sun he could fight this boy. It seemed impossible. The boy was way older than Peter, and on top of that, had better physical attributes. He had a fine physical frame and was way taller.

"Hey Pfidza, what happens to be the problem here?" Tumai, the school's head boy, asked the seventh-grade boy after having noticed the confrontation.

"Well, Blackface here thinks that he can challenge me."

"So what's so funny if he said he can take you? Maybe he can."

"Are you serious? Are you serious right now? I don't want to go to jail. If I fight him, I will kill this guy."

"If that's the case, then why don't you fellas settle this after school like real men?"

Surprised, Peter turned and faced the head boy, "are you suggesting that we should fight?" he charged.

"Hey, hey, hey, *mfana*, don't put words into my mouth. You are the one who uttered strong words. Sometimes you have to support what comes out of your mouth with real action, you know."

"Come on, give Blackface a break. He happens to be clever after all. He knows he won't win this. Don't you Blackface?" Pfidza taunted.

"I thought I told you earlier that I didn't like to be called that?" Peter rasped and turned to face Pfidza.

"I think I now agree with Tumai. We will settle this after school," Peter said.

Pfidza laughed. "You are so going to regret this," he said and shook his head.

"We'll see about that," Peter said and stormed off.

I immediately caught up with him in class at our desk. "Are you sure you are up for this?" I asked. "Do you really want to fight this guy?"

Peter seemed unperturbed. "That boy has a loudmouth," he said. "I am going to shut it today, and I am going to shut it for good."

I remained quiet, wondering what Peter was thinking. He could not fight Pfidza. That was suicide. Challenging Pfidza was like challenging everyone at the school. Pfidza was the school's top soccer striker and everyone at school adored him. That meant that no one would support Peter at the fight, well, no one, maybe except me. Was I going to support him? I asked myself. Though I wanted to be a good friend, nothing is more terrifying than going against a whole group of people when you are all alone. Was I brave enough to do that, to support Peter whilst everyone was supporting Pfidza? I wondered.

"You see, my friend," I cleared my throat and tried to reason with Peter. "Why don't you just go to Pfidza and apologise. It's not that hard, you know, you can tell him that the incident was just a small misunderstanding. I think he'll understand."

"What do you take me for? A coward?" Peter said. "I am going to thrash that bastard, and I am going to thrash him well."

I realised that this wasn't working. I was just wasting my time. I ended up shutting my mouth and waiting for the fight like everyone was doing. The wait didn't take that long. After school, we headed home. Having walked for a short distance, we noticed a group of people waiting for us. Pacing up and down in the middle was none other than Pfidza. He looked as if he couldn't wait for the fight any longer.

"Alright, alright, alright, now that everyone is here, let's now begin this," Tumai, the school head boy, said whilst rubbing his hands. He looked very excited. "So, how do you want to start? Oh, don't even bother answering that. I know how we should proceed."

He knelt and made two small mounds of soil. "Now, fellas, you know how this works. This mound here is Peter's mother's bosom," he said, pointing to one of the mounds. "This other one is the bosom of Pfidza's mum."

At that moment, Pfidza stepped forward and kicked the mound of soil that was meant to be the bosom of Peter's mom. Now one would wonder why something as stupid as this was of any significance. The thing is, in the Ndau culture, a mother is held in very high regard. The mother is the one who takes care of the children when the father is far away at work. She's the one who tends to her children when they are sick and cooks for them when they are hungry. From the moment a child is born, he or she creates a powerful bond with his or her mother. So kicking the mound was a grave insult. The moment Peter kicked the other mound, Pfidza immediately clinched his hands and launched himself at his nemesis.

"Kill him Pfidza! Kill him!" the crowd started cheering Pfidza. Pfidza swung his fist at Peter, but Peter jumped back, avoiding contact. Infuriated, Pfidza swung his fist again; this time, it landed perfectly on Peter's cheek, who then fell heavily on the ground. Seeing this, Pfidza immediately launched himself on top of Peter, pinned him to the ground and started punching him. When Pfidza had declared that he was going to 'kill' Peter, he hadn't lied. This wasn't a fight. It was complete carnage. The crowd was now hysterical and jeering Pfidza on.

I tried cheering Peter, but the noise of the crowd drowned my lone voice.

"Hit him Pfidza! Hit him!" They continued shouting at the top of their voices, jeering, clapping as they urged Pfidza on.

"Why are you all people cheering one person? That's not fair." Shungu, a boy who was in our class, finally complained. "Hey Peter, forget all these idiots, free yourself and thrash that bastard," he said and started cheering Peter.

By now, I had completely lost all hope. There was no way Peter was going to free himself from this, I thought. Well, I was wrong, Peter was far from being subjugated. From nowhere, he managed to land a powerful head-butt on Pfidza's face and another one a few moments later. Pfidza loosened his hold, and Peter freed himself and got up. The two immediately started exchanging blows again. One would have thought that after the hammering he had received, Peter would have been done by now, but no, that wasn't the case. He kept on fighting. Most people within the crowd who had been making a lot of noise had now fallen silent, surprised by Peter's resilience. As the fight progressed, the two fighters began to get tired.

Peter finally swung his fist upward, and his blow managed to land squarely on his opponent's chin. Blood gushed out, and a tooth fell out of Pfidza's mouth. It was the end of the fight. Pfidza covered his mouth and ran home. Seeing this, Shungu and I picked Peter up and hoisted him into the air. We were very happy. We felt victorious. Peter had done the impossible, defeating someone way older than him.

The euphoria about Peter's victory did not last long though, the news of the fight reached the school head the next day. Everyone who had been at the fight received severe thrashing and punishment. And Tumai, who had officiated the fight, was stripped off his position as head boy.

Even though we received severe punishment for our involvement, the incident did something to us. It made Shungu, Peter and I the very best of friends. We were now feared by the other boys. No one ever dared to challenge Peter or any one of us after the fight. On the weekends succeeding the fighting incident, the three of us spent a lot of time together. We would go hunting in the nearby hills, especially for rock rabbits, squirrels and birds. The area had a lot of them. They were many other bigger wild animals, like antelopes and wild boars, but we didn't go after them. They were far too fast for us. Wild pigs, in particular, were dangerous. If cornered, they could turn on their attacker with devastating effects. The area was also periodically invaded by predators, especially lions, which raided the villages, killing people's stock. We were aware of these predators, but we enjoyed the hunting activity all the same. I will have to admit that I was not a good hunter at first, but with time though I began to improve, partly due to some good advice from my Grandfather, and also due to help from Peter, who was already much experienced in the art of hunting. Peter had been taught by his father, a seasoned hunter and a former ranger of the Hwange National Park— so tracking animals was like second nature to him. I asked my Grandfather to make me a slingshot, one of the primary weapons in our hunting expeditions. Seeing how I enjoyed hunting, Grandfather agreed. He even went on to buy me two lion dog puppies.

I was thrilled to have the puppies. They were both males. One was a little bigger and had a shiny red wheaten coat with two small white spots on its left ear and right hind leg. I decided to call him Spot. The other one, which had a light wheaten coat and was a bit smaller, I named Cheetah. On the day I was given the puppies, with the help of Peter and Shungu, I was able to construct a small and comfortable kennel for the little dogs next to my hut. I didn't know it then, but these puppies would eventually become my closest companions.

Chapter 6

As he sat in his office Kam went through the events of the past month trying to figure out where it all went wrong. He had trusted John, and in his own opinion, he felt he had treated the man really well. Why then had John betrayed him? Could it be that John wanted more money? If this was about more money, why hadn't John said so? He wondered. Without warning, the phone began to ring, waking him from his troubling thoughts. Who could it be?

He wondered. He adjusted his chair and picked up the phone.

"Hello,"

"Hi Kam, It's me," Delight's deep voice leapt from the phone.

"Hey boss, how's it?" Kam replied nervously.

Delight laughed, "Boss? Really? I don't recall you ever calling me that before."

"It suits you," Kam declared.

"Okay, fine, let's cut the pleasantries, shall we? Have you talked to your man?"

Kam hesitated. "I've talked to him."

"And?"

"He refused, of course, he refused."

"Did you show him the photos?"

"I didn't."

"You didn't? Why?"

"I didn't want to scare him. I was afraid he would run. Maybe he still has some of the money."

Delight's voice immediately became cold, "I think I'll take care of this," he said.

"No, please don't. Let me handle this."

"Are you sure?"

"Yes, I am," Kam said with assurance.

"Okay," Delight said, "If you say so. Why are you being soft on him anyway?"

"I am the one who dragged him into this, so I feel responsible. If something were to happen to him, I would not forgive myself," Kam said.

Delight remained quiet.

"Are you still there?" Kam asked, looking at his receiver.

"I will be in touch," Delight said and hung up.

Kam sighed. One day everything is all calm. The next day, it's a storm. He looked at his watch and was surprised to see that it was almost seven. It was almost time to go home. He had not gone home last night and knowing his mother, he knew he would likely receive a scolding from her the moment he stepped into the house. He wasn't in the mood for that today. He had braced himself the whole day, thinking she would visit the shop, but surprisingly, she hadn't come. Something must have held her up. Fearing there might be an interrogation when he reached home, he decided to stay at the shop until ten. By that time, his mother would have gone to bed, he reasoned. He left his office and went into the main shop to see what was going on. There were many customers in the shop. Some were buying gadgets, while others were just checking the prices. Without saying anything to his employees, he started loitering around the shop, observing what they were doing. Two of them were serving customers whilst the senior employee, Mavis, explained to some elderly couple how a video cassette recorder worked. Even though everything was running smoothly, he remained in the shop observing the proceedings until it closed. When everyone had gone home, he finally went back into his office, where he briefly contemplated going to a bar but eventually decided not to, choosing instead to go through the books to pass the time. When he finally left the shop premises it was already past ten.

His mother, Eva, was still sitting in the living room watching the television when Kam arrived home. He was disappointed to find her still awake. He had thought she would have gone to bed by now. He had even tiptoed into the house, trying to make as less noise as possible, but alas, there she was, waiting for him.

"Hi mom, how was your day," he nervously greeted her, surreptitiously observing her face to see if she was angry. He was surprised to see that she was calm and not mad at all. "I can't complain. It was fine," she said.

"Is everything okay? Why are you still up?" he asked. "You are usually in bed by this time."

"Is that why you came late? To avoid me?"

"Oh no, not at all," he said, frantically shaking his head.

"Good, go and collect your food in the kitchen and come back here. I need to talk to you," she said, looking at him.

He went to the kitchen and came back with his food. "So what do you want to talk about, mom?" he asked, sitting down.

"I want to talk about us," she said. "You do realise that you and I are all that's left, right?"

"I know," Kam nodded.

"Really?"

"Yes, mother, I know."

"Good, so what's going on?"

"With what?"

"You."

Kam laughed, "Nothing, I am okay, I really am," he said. An awkward silence descended the room. Kam quickly lowered his gaze and focused his attention on his plate.

"I had an interesting talk with Tanya today," Eva finally said, breaking the silence.

"What did she say?" Kam asked.

"Nothing much, she was asking about you."

"What did she want?"

"Oh nothing really. She said you drove by her house yesterday."

Kam, who was about to swallow his food, almost chocked when he heard this but he nonetheless managed to maintain a poker face.

"What were you doing there?" Eva asked.

Kam stopped eating and put his plate down. "I don't know what your friend told you mom but I never went to her house?"

"So you are saying that she lied?"

"Well, maybe she saw a car that looked like mine, mom," he said, shifting uncomfortably on the sofa. He picked his plate and started eating again, focusing his attention on the plate. He could tell that his mother was now angry. She always became unusually silent when she became angry. Although he was avoiding looking at her, he could feel her flaming eyes fixed on him.

"I am tired," she finally said after lengthy moment of silence. "I am going to sleep."

"Good night," he called after her but she did not reply.

He looked at her as she went, feeling disgusted with himself for having lied to her. She knew he had lied, he thought with dread, she always knew. What he had done; denying he had been at Tanya's house, was it the right thing to do? He wondered. But even if he had admitted that it had been his car Tanya had saw, what reason would he have given for being at her house? He sighed and closed his eyes. These past days had been extremely stressful for him. Things weren't going the way he expected them to. He had put his confidence in John. Everything he did he had confided with him, yet despite all this, John had betrayed him. What made things even more complicated was that the bulk of the stolen drugs belonged to Delight, who, unfortunately, was baying for blood. If only the drugs were all his, the situation wouldn't have been this stressful. He would just have let John go or resolved the issue, in his own time. But why had John stayed after stealing? Why hadn't he fled? Kam wondered. Was he now with the police or he was just being stupid? He mulled the situation for a while and then decided he would confront John again the following morning. He would show him the condemning photos and he hoped John would finally confess and maybe even beg for forgiveness. Despite the painful betrayal, he still hoped he and John could resolve the issue of the missing drugs and go back to how things were. He needed John, even though he had become dishonest, John was still his only link with the vendors that sold his product on the streets.

From his mother's bedroom, he suddenly heard the sound of footsteps. Surprised that she was still up, he looked at the time. It was now approaching midnight. It was time, he realised, to go to his room to sleep. He didn't feel like getting up though, so he decided to remain on the sofa for a while. Staring blankly at the ceiling, he planned to the minute detail how he was going to confront John the next day.

Early the following day, he felt himself being shaken awake. When he opened his eyes he saw his mother standing beside the sofa, her concerned eyes staring at him.

"What time is it?" he asked as he rose from the sofa.

"Way past six. What happened?"

"Well, I decided to lay down a bit, and I just fell asleep."

"You have never done this before. Are you ok?" she asked. He could see that she wanted to continue last night's conversation.

"I am alright, mom," he said and quickly left the room before she could say anything else. He went to his room where he took clean clothes from the wardrobe and then rushed to the bathroom to clean up. Within a few minutes, he was on the road, heading for the flats. He went via the shop to collect the pictures he wanted to confront John with. The pictures were in the bottom drawer of his small office desk. Just as he entered his office, the phone rang.

"Hello," he answered.

"It's done," Delight's deep voice boomed from the phone.

"What? What's done?"

"Well, you know what they say? You can't make an omelette without breaking a few eggs."

"I don't understand," Kam said, confused.

"Don't worry, you will soon." Delight said and hung up.

Kam felt his heartbeat increasing. He swiftly drove to Mbare. When he was about to reach the flats where John lived, a police truck, full of armed police officers passed him. What was a truck full of armed police officers doing here? He wondered. He pulled over on the side of the road.

"Good morning, mother," he said to an elderly woman who was coming from the direction of the flats. "Sorry to bother you, but if I may ask, is everything okay? I saw a truck full of officers going the direction you are coming from."

"No, it's not okay at all," the woman said, shaking her head. "A man has been shot."

Kam felt his pulse rising again. He was now trembling and having a hard time breathing.

"When did this happen?" he finally asked.

"Around midnight, at least that's what I heard."

"So did you, by any means, hear the man's name? The man who was shot?"

The old woman stared at him suspiciously, "people who live at the flats said his name is John."

Kam did not ask any other question. He quickly drove back to his shop, where he locked himself in his office. Trembling, he sat in his chair and covered his face with his hands. It took him over an hour to calm his nerves. He even made a cup of tea and added a little pot in an attempt to calm himself. He was finding it difficult to accept what had happened. After a lengthy moment of intense pondering, he finally gathered the strength to call Delight.

"You killed him over forty kilos of weed? How could you do that?" he moaned, "I thought we agreed that I would take care of it."

"Oh, come on, don't be a wimp. It had to be done as a warning to others who may have been thinking of getting out of line. Don't worry too much about it, relax." Delight said and hung up.

Kam began trembling again. He got up and opened his window. He was now feeling feverish. He badly needed some fresh air. How could Delight sound so calm about all this? He wondered. Were those drugs really worth someone's life? This drug business wasn't at all what he thought it would be. He sighed and shook his head. How naive he had been. He was now beginning to realise what he had gotten himself into. He'd bitten more than he could chew.

Chapter 7

As they say, time moves relatively fast when all's well. Days turn into months, and before you blink the months turn into a year. For me, this could not be further from the truth. With the warmth and affection I received from my Grandparents, a whole year passed by without me even realising it. So despite my lack of comprehension of what it meant for me, I entered into the seventh grade— my last year of primary education. None of my friends had transferred to other schools, so I spent some of my free time with them, usually hunting. Being now familiar with many surrounding areas, I also wandered about with Cheetah and Spot. The dogs had now grown into hunting beasts. They were becoming so good that I believed they could even take out a small antelope on a good day, definitely not an easy task for a dog. They were loyal too. They followed me everywhere. The only time you saw me without them was when I went to school, and even then, I'd have to stop them from following me.

One Monday afternoon, as I came from school, I was surprised to see my mother's sister, Aunt Chipo, walking around the yard. This was her first visit since my mother's burial. As I approached to greet her, I heard someone crying. I greeted Aunt Chipo, who looked very sad and headed for the kitchen. As I neared the hut, I realised it was Grandma who was crying. She wasn't alone in the hut. She was seated on the floor near the fire while Grandpa and Aunt Chipo's husband sat on stools. Something terrible had happened, the atmosphere inside was gloomy.

"What's wrong?" I asked, looking at Grandfather.

"Mind your manners, boy, sit down," he said.

"I am sorry," I apologised, "I couldn't help but notice that Grandma is crying."

Grandfather remained quiet for a moment. When he eventually spoke, his voice was cracking.

"Tichakunda," he said, "It's about your Uncle."

"What about him?" I asked.

Grandfather looked at his feet, "we've just received word that he has passed away."

"Passed away?!"

"Yes, I'll have to go to Harare tomorrow to collect his body."

I was at a loss for words. I was shocked. Sitting there helplessly on the floor, with my Grandmother a few metres away, crying, I wondered why life at times could be so unfair.

What could be going on in the minds of my Grandparents right now? I wondered. They had lost their daughter not long ago, and now they had lost their only son. What made it even worse was that just like my mother, Uncle Mandikomborera had been murdered. According to the police report, he had been killed in a robbery incident.

Within a short space of time, our neighbours and the other villagers started to arrive. They all had consoling messages for my Grandparents. That night, my Grandfather and other close relatives and friends made travel arrangements to go to the capital to retrieve my late Uncle's body. The whole thing struck me deeply, more than I realised at the time. All the sad faces, seeing the body of my Uncle being interred in a hole on the ground, my crying Grandmother, and my helplessness were all too familiar. It was like being at my mother's burial once again.

After my Uncle's death, nothing was ever the same. His passing hit my Grandparents up to their core, particularly Grandfather. Just after the funeral, Grandfather started complaining about chest pains. He refused to go to the hospital, though. Grandpa was not a fan of hospitals. Whenever Grandma brought up going to the hospital, he would always say he was getting better. He was stubborn, my Grandpa, but you could tell he was sick. The old man was visibly losing weight.

"There's this healer who resides at Kondo. I've heard he is very good. Maybe you should visit him," Danda suggested one day to Grandpa when he had come to collect the cattle for grazing. Grandpa was sitting in the shade, making a cooking stick.

"Hey you, Danda," Grandma budged into the conversation before Grandfather could respond. "What kind of advice is that you're giving? Don't you see that he's sick?" she hissed. "What he needs is to go to the hospital."

"This healer you are talking about, is he that good?" Grandpa asked Danda, choosing to ignore what Grandma had just said.

Danda hesitated, "yes," he finally said. "I've heard that he is quite good."

"Well, I'll check him this weekend then."

Grandma momentarily stopped what she was doing and glared at Danda. She could not hide her disappointment. "Don't you think the time is ripe to visit a hospital?" she pleaded with her husband.

Grandpa remained adamant. "Why don't we try this healer first," he insisted, "if he is that good, maybe he will help me."

"But why go that far when the hospital is on your doorstep?" Grandma argued.

This time Grandpa didn't answer. He merely looked on the ground and then continued what he was doing.

Enraged, for a moment, Grandma looked hard at her husband and then at me, probably thinking that I would support her, but I didn't say anything. I just looked down. Later that day, Grandpa asked me if I could accompany him to Kondo to visit the traditional healer, catching me completely by surprise. I had never thought he would actually consider it, but looking at his face as he stood in front of me, I noticed the determination in his eyes. He truly wanted to go. Unable to come up with a reasonable excuse, I had no choice but to agree to go with him. I was also a bit curious, to be honest. Danda's assertion that there was a great healer who resided at Kondo had fascinated me. I wanted to see for myself if the so-called great healer would live up to the hype. Grandmother was not amused by the arrangement at all. She protested again to Grandpa, but her pleas fell on deaf ears.

There were no significant roads between Chikore and Kondo. Most of the people who travelled between the two areas usually did so by foot. It was quite a distance, but it was walkable. However, realising he would not walk the distance, Grandpa decided to use a scotch-cart. At around 5 AM the following Saturday, we began our journey to Kondo. Grandpa was nothing short of happy. If this healer was as good as Danda had said, then he was going to be okay in no time at all, he remarked along the way. I nodded and remained silent, absorbed by the scenery. The road we used passed through many homes. Having covered almost half of the distance, I finally realised that most of the people living along the way were underprivileged. Most of them seemed to be living from hand to mouth. Their homes were mostly composed of small mud-plastered huts, some which looked as if they were going to fall at any moment. Around the yards, you could see a dozen dirty youngsters running around, some of them half-naked. A couple of elderly men were already sitting outside in some homes, drinking home-brewed beer. The women were the only ones who were busy working. Some cleaned their kitchenware, some swept their yards and others were already returning from the river with buckets full of water on their heads. I was greatly impressed by these women. Most of them were working despite having babies on their back, others were even pregnant.

We reached the healer's homestead at around 10 AM.

It was an extensive homestead. I asked Grandpa why this was the case, and he told me that it was probably because the healer was a polygamist. Looking at his material possessions, one could easily tell the man was a successful traditional healer. He owned the largest herd of cattle I had ever seen. His cattle could have numbered to around two hundred beasts. Around the homestead, there were also several chickens and ducks which were loitering around the yard. When I counted his children, those I managed to count, they quickly surpassed twenty. Grandpa introduced himself and explained why we'd come. Upon hearing this, one of the healer's sons nodded and advised us to follow him. He took us to the healing quarters. When we reached the hut, the boy told us to wait outside. There were already other people inside who the healer was currently attending. After about fifteen minutes, they emerged from the hut, and we were finally allowed to go in.

When we went inside, I saw a sickly-looking, dirty and skinny old man sitting on a mat. He wasn't at all what I'd imagined. His feet were so cracked that I was confident a coin would fit easily in one of the cracks. Was this the famous healer? Was this the man who owned everything I had seen outside? I wondered. Grandpa started clapping as he uttered words of praise but the healer didn't respond. He glared at me and advised Grandpa that children were not allowed in his shrine. Grandpa nodded and instructed me to go outside. Though I didn't want to leave, I didn't protest. I walked out and waited for him outside. Grandpa remained inside the hut for almost half an hour. When he finally emerged, he looked contented. Things were now going to be okay, he said, his face beaming with hope. He even showed me some of the herbs he had been given. I nodded and listened to what he was saying, all the while wondering if those medicines really worked. I had doubts about the whole thing. I don't know why, but I had my doubts. I did not say anything to Grandpa, though. I remained quiet. I didn't want to ruin our journey which had gone so well.

In the following days, I began to worry about the exams, which were now just two months away. Peter, Shungu and I decided to use our free time to study. On some weekends, Peter and I would visit Shungu at his home to do maths questions; he was better at mathematics than I was. I struggled at calculating interest rate and long division questions. One of those weekends, having finished a group study, I was going home when I heard a familiar voice calling behind me. I was about a couple of hundred meters from our home.

"Hey there! Wait for me."

I turned back and saw Shorai running towards me. She was carrying a small sack on her head.

"What's that you are carrying?" I asked her when she reached me.

"Peas," she said, "my Aunt sent me to buy them. She likes peas a lot."

"How much do they cost?"

"Dollar per cup."

"Isn't that a bit expensive?"

"No. I think the price is quite fair. It's hard to get them in this area. That's why they are expensive," she said.

That made sense, I thought. "So what are you up to these days?" I asked.

"Well, nothing really. What about you?" she asked as she started walking very close to me. This struck me as odd. I began to feel very uncomfortable and moved away from her. She laughed.

"What's so funny?"

"Nothing," she said.

We walked in awkward silence for a couple of meters. "So, where are you coming from?" she finally inquired.

"From Shungu's homestead. I was there for a group study," I answered.

"Wow, I still can't believe you are about to finish seventh grade. You mean to tell me that next year we will be attending Chikore High together?"

"I think so," I said.

"That's so cool," she said, drawing closer to me again. I jumped back, "what's wrong with you today!" I exclaimed. "You are behaving strangely."

"I can whisper in your ear if you want to know."

"Please do," I said, lowering my head so I could hear what she had to say. What she did next surprised me. She kissed me on my cheek. I was still trying to get a grasp of what she had done when I was startled by a voice.

"Hey there, you two," the voice echoed. "What are you doing?" I turned to see who it was. It was Danda. Somehow, I felt very relieved when I saw that it was him. If it had been one of my Grandparents, what would I have said? Danda was chuckling. He seemed very amused by what he had just seen.

"So, what's going on here?" he asked, looking sharply at Shorai.

"Nothing," she said, "we were just talking."

"Oh really? Did you have to be that close to talk to him?" Danda asked.

Shorai did not reply. She just looked sharply back at Danda, turned and started walking towards her home.

Danda shook his head, "I need to talk with your Grandparents about that girl," he said.

I started panicking, "Danda, wait, let's talk about this."

"What do you want to talk about?" he asked.

"Don't tell them," I said, "Don't tell my Grandparents. We were just playing."

"Kissing, that's what you call playing?" he asked.

I didn't answer, I remained quiet, waiting to hear what he would say next.

"Do you know that she sleeps around with very old boys? And she's like what, fifteen maybe?" Danda asked with some seriousness in his voice.

"I didn't know that," I said.

Danda looked at me. I could tell from his expression that he knew I had lied. "Well, now you know. There are now a lot of ailments around these days, *mfana*. You are still very young. Behave yourself," he said.

"I will," I assured him. "So, are you going to keep this between us?"

Danda regarded me for a moment. "I will if you promise never to do what I saw you do with that girl ever again."

"I promise it won't happen ever again," I said pleadingly.

"Then it's settled," Danda said. "See you later at home then."

I went home thinking about what had happened earlier. Shorai had surprised me with her actions. She had left me wondering what she meant by what she had done. Maybe if Danda hadn't shown up when he did, I would have found out. I was beginning to regret the promise I had made to Danda. I wanted to see Shorai again. When she kissed me, I had felt something. It was a strange feeling I could not explain, one I had never felt before, one I desperately wanted to feel again.

Because of my thoughts, I reached home without even realising it. As I entered the gate to the homestead, my nose picked a pleasant aroma of chicken. I couldn't hide my joy when I entered the kitchen where my Grandmother was cooking. I was grinning from ear to ear.

"Good afternoon, Grandma." I greeted her as I sat down on the bench at the rear end of the kitchen.

"Good afternoon grandson, how are you?"

"I am fine, Grandma, I am fine. Where is Grandpa?"

"He is sleeping," she said as she removed her pot from the fire.

"At this time of the day? I've never seen him sleep in the afternoon. Is he okay?"

Grandma shook her head. "He is sick. He needs to go to the hospital."

"Why does he hate hospitals so much?" I asked, although I already knew what she was going to say.

"He is very old fashioned, grandson. He has always put his trust in traditional medicines," she said.

"Isn't there anyone who can change his mind?" I asked.

"Oh, do not worry yourself. He'll come around," Grandma said with a smile on her face. "By the way, how was your group study?"

"It was okay. I benefited a lot today."

"Good, you should work hard. Remind me after you have finished your lunch. I want to give you something," she said as she started dishing the food into plates. I was happy to see that she had cooked rice, my favourite. She handed me my plate, a generous portion of rice and two golden brown roasted pieces of chicken. The food was so delicious that I devoured everything she'd put in my plate, bones and all. After finishing my meal, I thanked her, went to my bedroom and laid on my bed. It was cool and refreshing inside. On the wall, two small geckos were busy chasing each other. I wasn't fond of wall creepers. Every time I saw one, I would always look for my broom. On this day though, I remained where I was, watching them with interest until they disappeared into the thatched roof. I had nothing important to do for the rest of the day, so I remained in the hut, daydreaming. Almost an hour passed before I finally remembered Grandma had asked me to remind her of something that she wanted to give me. I rose from my bed, went back to the kitchen and found her washing her cooking utensils.

"Hey Grandma, you said earlier that I should remind you of something you wanted to give me."

"Oh, that, wait here, I will go and get it," she said as she rose from where she was sitting. She came back a few minutes later, holding a plastic package with books in it. I was a bit disappointed.

This wasn't the 'something' I'd expected. I am not sure Grandma saw my frustration, and if she did, she didn't say anything.

She sat down and handed me the package, "these belonged to your mother. I thought you should have them," she said. At that moment, in a split of a second, my disappointment turned into surprise. I was utterly amazed by the condition that the books were in.

"You kept them all these years?" I asked.

"Of course I did. I always knew that they would come in handy one day."

"Thank you, Grandma," I said. "Thank you very much."

"Don't mention it, grandson. I hope they are going to help you in your studies. I hope they'll be your good luck charm."

"I hope so too," I nodded in gratitude.

I took the books back to my hut. As I closely examined them, I was happy to see that her handwriting at that time closely resembled mine. My mother was a good student. I could tell by the daily exercises that she wrote. She did well in all of them. Seeing her work did something to me. It gave me a sense of pride and hope. I told myself that I was going to try and emulate her. Lying there on my bed, I started reading all the exercise books, page by page. I must have overdone it. On the fifth book, I drifted off.

"Tichakunda!" I felt myself being shaken. I opened my eyes. Grandmother was standing beside my bed, crying.

"What is it, Grandma?" I asked her, rubbing my eyes.

"It's your Grandfather," she wailed. "His condition has suddenly worsened. I want you to go to Mr Sithole and tell him that I need his help. Your Grandfather needs to go to the hospital immediately. Please hurry, grandson, please, hurry!"

I ran to the Sithole homestead as fast as I could. Mr Sithole was one of the few people who owned a car in our village. Fortunately, when I reached his home, he was there. When I told him the message, he quickly got into his car, and we drove back home. Grandmother was anxiously waiting for us when we arrived, Danda too, having arrived after I had gone to the Sithole homestead. He, together with Mr Sithole, immediately helped Grandpa into the car.

"Grandson, I want you to behave yourself while I am gone, okay? Danda will stay with you until your Grandfather and I come back," Grandma said before she left.

"I will, Grandma, I will," I assured her.

"I hope so, and please, stay away from Shorai. Danda told me everything," she said as she got into the car.

I looked down and remained quiet. As they drove off, I waved them goodbye. When the car had finally disappeared down the road, I turned and angrily confronted Danda. "I thought you promised not to tell?" I hissed.

He shrugged his shoulders, "come on, *mfana*, you honestly expected me to believe that you were just going to stay away from that girl?'

"I meant what I said," I lied.

"Well, it does not matter now anyway. Whether you are lying or not, I am going to make sure that you keep that promise," he said, leaving me to digest his statement.

Still angry, I wobbled to my hut, where upon entering, I threw myself on the bed. What Danda had done, was it that unfair? I wondered when my anger began to fade. Deep within my heart, I knew that my anger was misguided. If Danda hadn't told on me, I probably would have rushed to see Shorai the first chance I would have had.

As the examination days approached, I increased my study intensity. Our grade seven teacher also kept us very busy during these days, calling us to school even on the weekends to revise past examination papers. All this time, I worried a lot about my Grandparents. Since they had gone, I had not heard from them. This, however, changed. A day before my exams, Grandma came back home accompanied by Mr Sithole. I was so happy to see her. She seemed to be in high spirits, and she told me that Grandpa was recovering well. He wished me the best of luck, she told me. Grandma however didn't stay long. After getting the provisions that she needed, she immediately went back to the hospital.

Even though it was for a brief moment, I was so happy that she had come. Her visit made it easier for me to write my exams, and I wrote them well. I was even pleasantly surprised when I encountered some of the questions that I had previously revised during my group studies. The happiness did not last long though, just a day after I had finished writing the exams, Grandma came back home, accompanied by Aunt Chipo and a couple of elderly women from the village. I sensed that something was terribly wrong. I was right; Grandpa had just passed away.

Chapter 8

After the passing away of Grandpa, I was beginning to see a pattern. I couldn't help but notice that there seemed to be an angel of death hovering over our home. I told my Grandma this, but she laughed it off and told me not to entertain such thoughts. Praying helps, though, if you have doubts about some things, she told me. So I prayed, day and night. I was assuring myself that everything would be okay. Everyone knows that we all need hope to handle the difficulties we face from one day to the next. What always enables us to forge on, despite the negativity that surrounds us, is hope. Hope for something, whatever it is. This was the hope I had. Nevertheless, death had other ideas.

In my first year in high school, seven months after Grandpa had passed away, Grandma followed him. The memory of her death is still vivid in my mind. People always say that happy memories will stay with you forever. That's true, but the sad part, though, is that the sad and painful ones will also haunt you for eternity—and I am afraid to say that's also true. To say I was devastated by my Grandmother's death is an understatement. There are instances where words aren't enough to describe a particular situation. The Shona people have a saying in their mother tongue, which roughly translates to, 'life is like a moving wheel.' It means that life rolls out episodes. Imagine a moving wheel, for example. Part of the wheel is pressed on the ground at any given time. But this is only for a short time. As it rolls, another portion of the wheel gets its turn to press on the ground. This sequence goes on and on. There is a time in life when one is unhappy, which is the season when your surface on the wheel of life is pressed hard on the ground. There is also a time when you are happy and rejoicing, and that's when your surface is not on the hard ground. That's life, they say. That is just how it works

I am not a sage, but I've seen people whose surface on the wheel of life has remained pressed hard on the ground. For them, the wheel of life has not moved at all. Circumstances seem to be reluctant to change for the better. For a moment, I wondered if I was one of those people. Things weren't getting any better. That winter, people in our village found something to talk about as they sat near the fire to chase away the cold. Everyone had an opinion. Some said my family was cursed, and others said my ancestors had done a terrible deed in the past and we were paying for it.

I felt very lonely during this time, apart from the unfortunate events that had befallen the family. Most of my friends and classmates had left to live elsewhere. Peter had gone to live in Mutare, and Shorai had eloped with some guy to Harare. They were even rumours she was pregnant when she left. Fortunately for me, though, Shungu had stayed. We had both enrolled at Chikore mission, and we were also in the same class. I spent a lot of time away from home with him during this time, hunting or just fooling around. It was a way to stay away from Aunt Chipo. After Grandma's death, she had come to live with me. My Aunt and I didn't get along. Living with her made me badly miss the days I had spent with my Grandparents. Unlike my Grandma, I found her to be officious and stingy. I was always complaining about this to Shungu, who eventually, maybe due to my continuous rumblings, suggested we find temporary employment during the school holidays for us to make a couple of bucks. Eager to earn my own money, I thought this was an excellent idea, and during the Easter holidays of our second year in high school, we found employment in one of the nearest tea estates, picking tea. It was a rough job and we made very little money, but I didn't care. Those days I spent working at the tea estates are some of my happiest, and I will always cherish them. They were a rare breath of fresh air. Away from the restrictions of our guardians and teachers, this was the time we started consuming alcoholic beverages. We did it secretly of course, being found out would have caused many problems and would have resulted in us being grounded. At the end of that holiday, I bought myself a second-hand FM radio. It was still in pretty good shape, and I was very proud of it. I could be forgiven for that. It was my first gadget. Alone in my hut, I would listen to either Radio 2 or Radio 3. These were my favourite radio stations. Radio 2 churned out local hits like *Chitekete* and *Shiri Yakangwara* by Leonard Dembo and Radio 3 played the fast-paced international hits of the day. When I was bored of listening to the radio, I would sometimes go fishing in the Nyagadza river with my two cousins. I was now quite good at it. The only sad thing was that Uncle Mandikomborera wasn't there anymore to witness how proficient I had become.

My Aunt made a lot of changes when she came, many of which I found distasteful. One decision that particularly didn't go down well with me was the termination of Danda's employment. I had grown extremely close to him, and regarded him as part of the family. After sacking Danda, my Aunt went on to sell all the cattle. Some of the cattle she sold were cattle that Chisvo's relatives had paid as part compensation for my mother's death. Before he passed away, Grandfather had expressly told me that these cattle belonged to me and would be used for my education. I did not say anything when she sold the cattle. I didn't want to seem unappreciative. After all, Aunt Chipo was paying my school fees and taking care of me. The least I could do was keeping my mouth shut and being grateful for what she was doing for me. Just when I was getting used to the existing state of affairs, something happened. It was during the middle term of my third year in high school. My Aunt's husband announced he was going to South Africa. His relative, who was already living there, had found him a job. My Aunt decided to go with him. This shocked and frightened me a bit, but not for long. By now, I had spent a lot of time away on temporary work during the school holidays and this had taught me how to live alone. I had always felt alone anyway. Truth be told, when we were living together, I had always been the odd one out. Every time an argument had broken out at home, no one had ever been on my side.

One Friday afternoon, about a month or so after my Aunt and her family had left, I heard the dogs bark as I lay on my bed listening to the radio. I immediately ran outside to see who it was.

"Hey! Call off your dogs before they bite me," a young woman standing at the edge of the yard called out to me. She had a long stick in her hand, which she was furiously swinging at the dogs. I quickly chided the dogs. For a moment, I wondered who the young woman was, but after closely looking at her face, I finally recognised her.

"Oh my god, it's you!" I exclaimed.

Shorai laughed, "of course it is I. Who did you think it was?"

"You have changed!" I exclaimed.

She smiled, and then her face suddenly became serious. "I heard about your Grandparents. I am so sorry."

"Well," I shrugged, "some things do happen. It can't be helped."

She nodded, and we fell silent for a moment.

"So what's up? The last time I heard about you, people were saying you were pregnant and had run off with some guy." I blurted out. For a few seconds, her face turned sort of funny.

"You just couldn't resist, could you?" she finally said, giving me a weak smile.

I shrugged, "I am a curious person. One has to ask sometimes."

She glanced away for a moment before looking at me again. I looked at her face, and she looked away, then looked at the ground and started kicking pebbles. She raised her head and looked at me again. This time her eyes were watery.

"It's my fault," she said. "It's true what they say, I was indeed pregnant, but I suffered a miscarriage. After I lost the baby, I realised that the guy I was with wasn't the person I thought him to be, so I eventually left him."

I kept looking at her. She was now crying. I was a bit surprised by this and I didn't know what to do. Without thinking, I moved closer to her and gently placed my hand on her shoulder.

"I am very sorry to hear this," I consoled her. She didn't say anything. She just put her hand on top of mine and looked at me. I froze, not knowing what to do next. In that instant, Spot started barking, so I stepped away from her and moved towards the dog to see what it was barking at. It was nothing dangerous really, just some chameleon trying its best to navigate across the yard.

"What is it?" Shorai asked, closely standing behind me.

"Just a small chameleon, can you believe that? From the way the dog was barking, I thought maybe it was something dangerous, like a snake," I said. Shorai did not say anything, choosing to maintain a distance between herself and the chameleon. She seemed to be genuinely terrified of it.

"I'm going home," she finally said.

"So soon?"

"Yes, there are some things I need to sort out there."

"Thanks a lot for coming to see me," I said.

"Don't mention it; that is what friends do," she said with a smile.

I waved at her as I watched her go. After walking for a couple of meters, she turned.

"Tichakunda," she called.

"Yes."

"Would you care to accompany me to the river tomorrow?" she asked.

"Why?"

"I am afraid to go alone."

I almost laughed loudly. "Unless something important comes up tomorrow, I don't see why not," I finally said.

"Thanks."

I watched her go. How about that, she wanted me to accompany her to the river. Why? The excuse that she was afraid was total crap. But then again, I had many dirty clothes that needed washing— a heap of them. I wasn't fond of washing clothes, so I had always deferred washing them. After thinking about it, I felt that maybe it wasn't such a bad idea. After all, who knows, perhaps she was just fooling around with me. She came that Saturday, apparently she wasn't joking. I took my clothes, and we headed for the river. Like a faithful hound, I closely followed behind her— half listening at her chattering while furtively gazing at her mound. The whole journey to the river was ocular manna; a pleasure dished so generously. By the time we reached the river, I had already been enthralled. She insisted on washing my clothes, and I was more than willing to let her. She chatted continuously about her life in Harare. She wanted me to go with her someday, she said. Go with her? I laughed, believing that she was joking, but as the day progressed, I began to realise that she was actually serious. She told me that she owned a store where she sold fruits and vegetables. It was very profitable, she said, and with my help, we could turn it into a big business. I remained quiet and listened while she continued with her rumbling. After washing the clothes, we eventually returned home, with Shorai still talking about how cool the city was. When we reached home, I entered my hut where I wanted to put back the bucket I had used to carry my clothes to the river. She followed me inside and made some remark about how my hut was so clean and organised. I grinned happily like a young boy offered candy.

"I am going home," she said, drawing near and kissing my cheek. I completely lost control of myself after that. By the time I finally came to my senses, we were both lying on my bed, breathless.

Chapter 9

He found his mother in the kitchen. She was standing at the sink, busy washing her utensils. When she saw him coming in, she briefly stopped what she was doing and turned to look at him.

"How did it go?" she asked

Kam smiled, He had known she would ask. Ever since he admitted to her that he was seeing Susan she always asked how things were going. "It went well, mom," he said. "We had lunch, and after that, I took her to Eastgate to see a movie."

"That's so sweet. Which movie did you see?"

"Forever Young."

"Did Susan like it?" Eva queried.

"She seemed to like it."

"I am so happy for you two," Eva said. She looked happy, she was smiling.

"Thanks mom," Kam said as he walked to the fridge. He poured himself a glass of juice and headed to his room.

In his room, Kam sat on his bed and closed his face with his hands. He felt mentally tired and depressed. The past months had been difficult for him. At night he found himself being terrorised by nightmares, he wasn't sleeping well.

For almost six months, he'd now managed to disregard and avoid Delight. All his calls at the shop were now being received by Mavis, whom he'd expressly instructed to tell Delight that he was not around every time the drug kingpin had called. He had even managed to avoid Maromo, Delight's right-hand man, although he wasn't sure how long he could keep this up. He was now tired of always having to look over his shoulder. His only hope now was that they would eventually leave him alone. John's death had deeply shook him. Of course he had known that Delight and his people would go after John but he hadn't thought they would kill him. He only expected them to rough him up a bit. Because of his stupidity, he was now an accomplice to murder. Kam sighed and shook his head. It was no use crying over spilt milk now. What had been done had already been done.

The next day, Kam stuck to his daily routine —staying in his office for the greater part of the day, venturing into the shop only when he felt he was urgently needed. Being a weekend day, many people were coming in. From his office, Kam could faintly hear their indistinct chatter. At around 2 pm, as he was busy mulling over the events of the previous day, one of his subordinates, TK, came running into his office.

"What's wrong?" Kam asked, surprised by the intrusion.

"There is a man in the shop who says he wants to see you."

"I thought I clearly instructed you to tell anyone who came looking for me that I wasn't around."

TK hesitated, "you did, sir, but..."

"But what?"

"The man, sir. He won't go."

Kam jumped out of his chair, now feeling a bit unsettled. "What does he look like?" he asked.

"He is a huge fellow, probably in his mid-forties. He's wearing fancy clothes," TK paused, thinking. "Oh, and he annoyingly seems to be fond of his beard."

Kam missed a pulse. That had to be Delight. "You know what," he said as he dusted the empty visitors' chair. "Let him in."

"Are you sure?"

"Yes. Let him in."

He sat in his chair, not knowing what to expect. Why had the drug kingpin come? What did he want? He pondered. When Delight came in, Kam was caught off-guard. The man seemed to be in high spirits. He put the satchel he was holding on one of the visitors' chairs and gave Kam a warm brotherly embrace as if nothing unusual had happened. Not sure what to make of this, Kam decided to go along with the charade. Things seemed to be going well for Delight, Kam noticed. The man looked well taken care of, he looked healthy. After a couple of minutes of nattering, Delight finally opened the satchel. He drew a bundle of cash and placed it on the table.

Kam stared at the money. "What am I supposed to do with this?" he asked.

"I want you to go to Gondola. A large consignment has just arrived there."

"You want me to go to Mozambique?"

"Is there a problem?" Delight asked, suddenly looking very grave.

Kam hesitated, he wanted to tell Delight there and then that he wasn't interested anymore, but he couldn't bring himself to say it. "I guess it's all right," he finally said. "Isn't Maromo more suited for this job, though?" he asked.

"You are both going," Delight said, reaching into his pocket for a packet of cigars. "Maromo alone will attract a lot of attention, but with you accompanying him, this will make things easier. That's what we agreed with our friends at the border."

Kam stood up, rubbing his face and started pacing around the room. "When is this supposed to happen? Do you realise that I'll have to lie to my mother, again?"

Delight puffed his cigar as if it was the most important thing to do at that time. "Well, I am sorry about that. You'll just have to come up with a good excuse. Maromo will pick you up here at 3 am tomorrow."

Kam leaned on the wall and looked on while his associate puffed away at his cigar, patting his beard lightly as he did so. TK had been right, Kam thought. It was indeed rather annoying. For a moment, he considered his options. With this man, he knew he needed to tread carefully. Delight was a dangerous man. Someone who could kill to get what he wanted. Precisely how many people had this man killed? And how many more would he kill to achieve what he wanted to achieve? Kam pondered. And if Delight was to suddenly turn against him, would he be able to defend himself? Kam wondered. He dreaded the answer, but he knew it. If his unpredictable associate decided to turn against him, there would be little he could do to save himself.

Delight finally stood up, "let me show you the ride you will use," he said, walking out of the office. Kam nodded and followed. Outside, Maromo was standing beside a Toyota 4runner. Kam examined the car for a couple of minutes while Delight explained how the journey would be carried out. After everyone had been satisfied with the arrangement, Delight and Maromo drove off.

"How did you manage to convince him, boss?" Maromo asked after they had driven for a few minutes.

"I didn't do anything. The boy is clever. He knows his life depends on it."

"Does it?"

"Well, he can't just quit after all we have been through. Are you forgetting that we even took care of his idiot for him?"

Maromo did not say anything, choosing instead to keep his eyes on the road.

"Talking about taking care of things, if he gives us problems, would you have issues getting rid of him?"

"Who? Kam?" Maromo asked, surprised.

"Yes."

"No boss, no," he said after a moment of thought. "You know me. There won't be any problems at all?"

"Good," Delight said. For a moment they drove in silence.

"So, is there a place I can find a lady who wants to have fun?" Delight asked.

Maromo's jaw dropped, "Huh?"

"A lady. You know what I am talking about. Do you know where I can find one?"

"Well, I know a place," Maromo said with hesitation.

"What are you waiting for then? Take me there."

Maromo nodded and turned the car towards the red light district of Harare, the Avenues area. This is an area where those who crave wanton carnalities flock to. Maromo being one of these people, knew this place very well. He drove to a flat which he knew housed many ladies of the night. When he reached the flat, many young women were sitting outside in the shade, possibly gossiping. Not knowing what to do next, Maromo stopped the car and looked at his boss.

"Wait here," Delight remarked and got out of the car. He walked towards the women and started conversing with them. A minute or so later, he returned, a pleasingly plump young woman behind him, and instructed Maromo to drive them to the Sheraton Hotel.

Maromo didn't waste time. He sped towards the hotel, dropped off Delight and his lady friend and headed home. Half an hour later, he was parking the car in front of his rented St Mary's house in Chitungwiza. His boss had expressly instructed him not to fool around with the car since it carried some very important goods. Maromo recalled the moment. He'd been shocked when his boss opened a hidden compartment behind one of the seats.

"Do you think he will agree to this?" he had asked after having seen what was inside.

Delight had paused, "I don't think he will," he'd said after a moment of thought. "He doesn't have to know. Let's keep him in the dark until the exchange. After that, well, we will cross that bridge when we reach it."

Maromo looked at his watch; it was 4.10 pm. He needed to rest. He had a long journey tomorrow. He stayed in the car, looking at the front door, dreading to get in. The thing is, Maromo had come to despise the woman on the other side of that door, and, as if that wasn't enough, he feared her as well. All that and yet she had managed to have seven children with him. Maromo cursed himself. How could he have let that happen? He asked himself. He knew the answer though, things hadn't always been this way. Once upon a time, she had been a fine girl. That's until she decided to have water as her totem. All his emotions for her had now all drained away, like water from a leaking tank, but he couldn't get rid of her now; she had a solid case on him. She knew all of his dealings. Maromo sighed and got out of the car. He needed a cold bath and some good sleep urgently. He opened the door, and there she was, sitting on the sofa, watching television.

Maromo sneaked in the most convincing fake smile he could muster. "Hi honey. Where are the kids?" he asked, heading straight for the bedroom door.

His wife, mistaking this for an invitation, coyly smiled back. "They have gone to play," she replied.

Maromo looked in horror as she stood up, apparently to follow him. Feeling trapped, he rubbed his head. He needed to think of an excuse to get rid of her, fast. He frowned. "Hey honey, could you please go buy me some painkillers at the shops? My head is killing me," he said, reaching for his pockets and handing her a couple of notes.

His wife froze for a moment, confused, but being eager to please, she finally took the money and rushed to the shops. Maromo breathed a sigh of relief. He was alone at last. Finally, he could have that cold bath which he urgently needed.

Chapter 10

When Delight and Maromo left, Kam remained standing in front of his shop, angry with himself. This had been his chance to tell Delight that he was now done with this drug business, but he had been afraid to take it. Now that he had squandered the opportunity, what was he going to do? He walked to his car. All this excessive thinking wasn't getting him anywhere. He needed to live a little. He needed something to cheer him up. Maybe visit Susan at her work and then take her to a nice dinner. Who knew what would happen after that. However, the problem was that Susan seemed not yet ready to take the relationship to a new level. He wasn't even sure she was that liberal. By the way, when was the last time that he'd had any real fun? He wondered. The woman at the little bar! He smiled as the vivid memory of the lady came back to him. How could he forget? Would it hurt if he saw her again? He didn't think so. In any case, no one would find out. Jingling his keys, he immediately got into his car and headed for Mbare.

There was a lot of traffic on the road. The hour hand had just left the fourth digit, and many people, having finished work, were now heading home. Kam watched with indifference as kombis full of passengers sped past him. They were ferrying people who lived in Mbare, Glen Nora and other nearby suburbs. Just before the Rotten Row flyover, he noticed a lot of cars were parked on the side of the road. An accident had just occurred. A commuter omnibus had crashed into the rear of a private car. This didn't surprise him at all; it always happened in the city. Like every driver who was passing through, he slowed down and peeped through his window. It didn't seem as if there had been fatalities from what he was seeing, but some people had been injured. Police officers, possibly from Harare

Central Police station, were already at the scene. An ambulance had also arrived to ferry the wounded to the hospital.

A few moments later, Kam reached the little bar. A strong smell of cigarettes and booze hit him the moment he stepped inside. The little bar was rammed with ladies and gents who were soothing their throats. The television was on, and many people had their eyes glued to the screen. Some of them turned their heads and gazed at him suspiciously, wondering what he was doing in there, but he ignored them and headed for the counter. Behind it stood a tall lady with an amazingly long neck. She was leaning over the counter, her hand on her cheek, chewing some gum. She seemed extremely bored.

"Hi," Kam greeted her as he approached the counter.

"Hi," she replied, smiling.

"I am looking for someone," he said and then described the woman he was looking for.

"She doesn't work here anymore," the tall lady replied, looking not even a bit interested in what he was asking. Some gentleman who had been sitting at the back approached the counter and stood beside Kam. From the way he was acting, he seemed to be the lady's boyfriend. Kam gazed at the fella and didn't see anything to be frightened about. He ignored the man and continued questioning the lady.

"Do you know where she lives?" he asked. The lady shook her head. Kam sighed, this wasn't good. This wasn't good at all. His plans for the next few minutes had suddenly gone down the drain. Now what? He wondered. For a moment, he thought of buying a beer, but he eventually decided not to. He had a long outing the next day, he needed to rest. Perhaps a good night sleep would do him good. Kam decided to go home.

He got into his car and headed towards Belvedere, driving slowly to give himself time to compose an excuse for his likely absence the next day, one which he felt would be convincing to his mother. When he finally reached home, he found her in the kitchen, preparing supper.

"You came early today," she remarked.

Kam smiled warmly, "yes, mother, I did," he said.

"You wouldn't mind helping your mother, would you?"

Kam thought about it. This was probably a good time for him to announce that he would not be around the next day, so he stayed.

"Mom."

"Yes, my son."

He hesitated. "Well, tomorrow, I will not be around. I am going to Mutare to check how things are going. I don't want to sleep there, so I think I might leave very early."

"How early?"

"Maybe at three."

His mother paused what she was doing. "Dean, I thought we were a team," she said.

"We are mother. We are a team," Kam said reassuringly.

"So when are you planning to show me that shop of yours?"

"Soon, mother, I'll go with you one day, I promise. It's just that there is still some work which needs to be done."

"Some work which still needs to be done? But what about all that money you have been banking? Isn't that money coming from that shop?"

"It is, that's actually the reason I want some work to be done there. I will take you there one of these days, mother, I promise," Kam said.

The next day Kam woke up early. A glance at his watch showed him it was now only a minute to three. He was going to be late. He quickly rushed to the shower, and after a quick bath, he dressed and drove to his shop. When he arrived, Maromo was standing beside the car, already waiting for him.

"You're late," he remarked.

"So?"

"Do you know how important this is? Boss said these suppliers are new. So we have to be there on time."

"Hey, relax, I woke up a little late, okay? If you are so concerned about arriving late, then I suggest you take less time on the road. This seems to be a very capable car," Kam said as he opened the door of the 4runner. Maromo shook his head. He hated people who didn't show up on time. This journey was important and time was of the essence. He took the A3 highway and sped along towards the Mozambique border. By 6 am, they had already reached Penhalonga, a mining town 254 km South-East of Harare. When the clock struck 9, they were already inside Mozambique's Manica province, driving towards Gondola. Kam felt relieved, the journey had gone well. Just like Delight had said, they found a red truck parked in front of a post office.

The car had one man in it. They approached it and parked beside it. After getting acquainted with the man, Maromo and Kam drove closely behind him to a concrete fenced house. The man introduced them to their suppliers. After the introductions, Kam did not waste time. He immediately demanded to see the product. Two men brought into the room fourteen sacks of weed. Kam briefly checked one of the sacks and then signalled Maromo, who stepped forward and checked the whole batch. Having been satisfied with the product, Maromo made the Ok sign and they proceeded with the transaction. As all this was happening, there was a man who remained quiet, watching the proceedings. Kam didn't give the man much thought, concentrating on closing the deal. When the transaction was finally completed, Kam was surprised when the man stood up and asked if he had brought something.

"What are you talking about? Who are you?" he asked.

The man ignored the questions. "Mr Delight promised that you would bring me something," he said.

Kam shook his head. "I don't know what you are talking about," he said.

"We have your things," Maromo finally interjected. Kam turned and faced Maromo, surprised by what his companion had just said.

"Follow me," Maromo said to the man and went outside. The man followed with Kam close behind him. Maromo walked to the 4runner, opened the door and adjusted the seats. Kam could hardly hide his dismay when Maromo opened a compartment hidden behind the adjusted seats. It was full of rhino horns, there were four of them. The man inspected the horns. "Mr Delight is a man of his word," he remarked, looking very pleased.

"Well, since we have held our end of the bargain, I suppose you have something that belongs to us?" Maromo said.

The man smiled. "Of course, follow me," he said as he walked to a van parked a few metres away. He went to the back of the van, opened it and pulled out what looked like Pizza boxes.

They were two of them. Maromo took one and opened it. It was full of money. US dollars.

Using a portable money counter he had brought with him, Maromo counted the money while Kam looked on. Satisfied that everything was there, Maromo took the money and handed the man his horns. While all this was happening, Kam could hardly contain himself. His face burned with anger. He didn't say anything, though. He knew fully well that causing a commotion wasn't going to get him anywhere. The whole journey back home, Kam remained silent, thinking. How could Delight hide this from him? How could he do this? Did Delight think of him as a partner, or he was just some pawn in his game? He pondered. When they finally arrived back in Harare, they drove to Maromo's house, where they dropped off their merchandise and then headed to Kam's shop. By now, it was way past midnight. When they reached the shop, they found a taxi parked outside. Kam was about to approach it and ask the driver what he was doing there when Delight emerged from the car.

"Did everything go well?" he asked, grinning as he approached Kam.

"You are truly one rotten son of a bitch, do you know that?" Kam said, suddenly getting furious.

"I am so sorry, that's why I waited for you here, to apologise. Can we go somewhere more comfortable, where we can talk?" Delight asked.

Kam reached into his pocket and pulled the spare keys for the shop. He was tired now, but anger got the best of him. Curious to hear what Delight had to say, he led his fellow associate into his office.

"Do you know how many years you will spend in jail if you are caught with a rhino horn?" he asked once they had comfortably settled.

"One can only imagine."

"And yet you have the nerve to let someone carry four for you without even informing them?"

"I am sorry," Delight said, looking contrite.

"But why didn't you tell me? Why did you do that?"

"You might not want to hear this, but the thing is, you are still a virgin when it comes to this business. I thought that you would panic if I told you about the horns, and judging from how you are reacting now, it's safe to say that my presumption was correct. What I did was necessary. Sometimes you need balls like hard-boiled eggs for you to make it in this business."

"Really? If you are so bold, why didn't you travel with me to Mozambique?" Kam asked.

Delight scratched his head, "look, I know you are angry, I apologise. Something like this will never happen again, I promise."

Kam remained quiet, looking at Delight.

"You are now making me nervous," Delight said after a moment of silence.

"Can I ask you something?" Kam said.

"What do you want to know?" Delight said.

"Have you ever considered eliminating me in the event that things go sour?"

Delight froze, visibly taken aback by the question.

"Well?" Kam charged.

"Wait here," Delight said, exiting the room. He came back after a moment with an envelope which he threw at Kam.

"What's this?" Kam asked.

"Your cut," Delight said. "You see, this is all one big misunderstanding. I will never do anything to hurt you, my friend. I will never do anything like that."

Chapter 11

The first time Shorai asked me to go with her to Harare, I didn't take her seriously. I thought she was just joking. How could I not? She was asking me to leave school and go with her to someplace I had never been. I would never have considered going to Harare, but after that dance with her, my first one, I became disoriented. The whole experience was so intense, and being young, a novice in all matters with regards to women, I quickly crumbled. Shorai was good, extremely good. In the following days, she cooked, washed my clothes and acquainted me to some very licentious rites. She made me feel very special and treated me like a prince. Having grown so lonely, everything she did left me so overwhelmed that I ended up agreeing to go with her in spite of myself.

On the date we had agreed, Shorai and I secretly took off and boarded a bus to Chipinge. From there, we boarded another one which took us to Harare. This was my first time seeing the city, and when we arrived at Mbare bus terminus, I couldn't help the fascination. The place was pulsating with life. It was a lot noisier than I had expected, with a lot of traffic and many people moving back and forth, searching for transport to various destinations. There were many vendors around, both men and women, selling various wares. Most of the goods being sold were snacks, soft drink, fresh fruits and vegetables, but I also saw stores which sold tools, small grains, trinkets and assortments of herbs that the sellers declared could cure various ailments.

The room Shorai rented was much more comfortable than I had anticipated, and the house was conveniently located near the market. We shared the house with other two tenants, a single mother of two and a middle aged fellow who worked as a tout at Mbare bus terminus. I quickly warmed up to both of them. They were very friendly, and they did not ask a lot of unnecessary questions. Once settled, we immersed ourselves in the vending business. Every morning, we would wake up very early to wait for the trucks that supplied us with our wares. The trucks came from the surrounding plots that farmed fruits and vegetables. We bought these in bulk and then sold them to our customers in small portions. The business did not make us a lot of money, but I wasn't bothered much. I had Shorai, that's what mattered to me.

About a month after we had left Chipinge, I was approaching our house one day when I saw a car that looked familiar parked in the front yard. I walked closer and examined it. It looked exactly like Mr Sithole's. Could it be him? I wondered as I walked towards the front door. The moment I walked into the house, my suspicions were finally confirmed. Sitting in the dining room, which we shared with all the other tenants, were Mr Sithole and Shungu. I was a bit jolted when I saw them. Although the car parked outside had raised my suspicions, seeing them in person in that room struck terror into my heart. The mood in the room was charged, extremely hostile, which might be the reason why all the other tenants had locked themselves in their rooms. Mr Sithole looked very livid, Shungu too. When I turned to look at Shorai, my heart wept for her. She sat huddled at the far end of the room, looking terrified. The humiliation, and the hurtful words she might have endured before I arrived, I could only imagine. Without saying anything, I finally walked across the room and sat beside her.

"I am very disappointed in you young man," Mr Sithole said without even giving me time to settle and greet him.

I remained quiet. I had not expected this. His visit had taken me completely by surprise. What did he want? And how had he managed to find where we stayed? I wondered.

"I want you to pack all your things right now," he said, his voice hoarse with anger.

"What! Why?" I said.

"Tichakunda, my friend, we need to go back home, back to school. Everyone in class is worried sick about you," Shungu implored.

"I am not going anywhere. I am okay here where I am."

Mr Sithole gave a very long and sarcastic laugh when I said this

"Young man, this is not a negotiation, you are going back home today, whether you like it or not."

"No, I am not going anywhere," I stubbornly declared.

Mr Sithole stood up, now more furious than ever. "What did you say, boy?" he hissed, glaring at Shorai and me. Shorai shrunk further in her seat, terrified.

"Let me talk to him," Shungu finally said, probably sensing that things were about to escalate.

He took my hand and led me outside.

"What's gotten into you Tichakunda? I thought we had plans? Going to college and stuff?" he said.

I did not reply him. I looked on the ground to avoid his gaze. We stood for a while in silence.

"That girl seriously did something to you, I am sure of it," Shungu finally said, starting to sound dejected.

Feeling uncomfortable with what he was saying, I started walking away from him.

"Where do you think you are going?" he shouted after me. I did not respond, instead, I increased my pace.

"Tichakunda! Stop!" Shungu shouted again. I turned and looked back. Mr Sithole had now come out of the house. Both him and Shungu were now running and following me. This alarmed me. I started running towards the market, a place where I knew they would never find me. When I got there, I quickly mingled with other people. I am not sure when Mr Sithole and Shungu finally gave up looking. They never found me. I did not return home that night. I decided to go to Victor's house. He was one of the vendors I had befriended in the past few days. We had quickly become friends because he was about my age, and like me, he had also prematurely left school. He stayed with his mother and made a living by selling fruits and vegetables at the market. When I told him the situation I was in he agreed to help and gave me a place to sleep that night. The next day, I waited for Shorai at our small store, thinking that she would show up, but she didn't. After loitering around the marketplace to pass the time, I finally returned to the house later that day. I found her cowered in our room, still visibly shaken and waiting for me.

"What happened? Have they left yet?" I asked, holding her hands and pulling her close to me.

She shook her head. "I don't know."

"What do you mean you don't know?" I asked, now feeling confused.

"When they started chasing you, I knew they would never find you. So I fled before they came back. I was afraid. Mr Sithole had threatened to beat me up before he had gone after you," she said, looking at me. Her eyes were red. She must have been crying earlier, or perhaps she had not slept at all last night. "Maybe you should go back," she suggested.

"Are you crazy? How can you even say that?" I asked, surprised by what she had just said.

"I am afraid. You do realise that I am older than you, right?"

"So?"

"What if they go to the police?"

I shook my head. "That's not going to happen," I said. At that moment, someone knocked at the door. We both remained quiet for a moment, wondering who it was.

"Shorai, it's me. Can I come in?" a voice called. It was Tendai, one of the tenants we shared the house with. We all called her Tindo for short. Shorai was very close to her and treated her more like her own mother. I sat on the bed as Shorai offered Tindo a chair to sit on. After the visitor had comfortably sat down, Shorai then came back and sat close to me.

"So, how are you two coping?" Tindo asked.

"We are okay," Shorai replied. "We're a bit shaken, but we're okay."

"You two are something else. Why didn't you tell me that Tichakunda was still going to school?" she asked, looking at Shorai.

Shorai shrugged, "I didn't think that it was important to mention."

"From what I heard from that man, Mr Sithole, who came to get Tichakunda, people back home are not happy at all. You might want to reconsider your decision Tichakunda," she declared. Shorai and I looked at each other and remained quiet.

"Well, I hope this is not just some phase of infatuation, because if it is, trust me, one of you is in for some bitter regret," Tindo said.

"It's not like that," Shorai said, drawing closer to me and placing her head on my shoulder.

"This is not just some infatuation. I love him."

I literally melted when she said that. Tindo folded her hands and looked at us. Her face was portraying an expression I could not fathom. I did not bother myself asking why she was looking at us like that. Why could I? I was happy, happy with Shorai, happy with where I was. When I went back to the market later that day, Victor was eager to hear what had transpired.

"So, tell me the news. What happened?"

I smiled weakly. "Nothing worth mentioning. They've gone."

"And you are sure that they are not coming back?" he asked.

"Yes, I am," I lied.

"That man, though, he really is concerned about your welfare. Do you realise that?"

"How would you know that?" I asked.

"Man are sometimes blind to what's right in front of them but they aren't blind to what's in front of others. I'm not the one involved in this so I have better perspective," Victor said.

I remained silent, thinking about what he had said.

"That girl of yours, though, is she worth it, my brother," he asked.

"She is," I declared, "she really is, and I love her."

"I know you do. Otherwise, why would you leave school to come here with her? I am just wondering if your girl is sincere on her part."

"Everything is fine. I trust Shorai," I said.

"Well, if you say so," Victor said and focused his attention on the woman who was approaching him. A teenage girl stopped in front of my store and looked at what I was selling. She hesitated and then moved on. I turned and looked at the people walking back and forth behind me. Something was troubling me. Was Mr Sithole going to return? I wondered. If he did return, what was I going to do? For the next few days, Shorai and I were very alert, expecting that Mr Sithole would come back at any moment, but to our relief, nothing like that happened. After about a month, we finally felt reassured that he was not going to return. Life went on. We continued our vending business, all the while hoping that an incident like this would never happen again.

Chapter 12

The year 98 started well for Delight and company. This is despite the fact that the economic situation around the country was starting to get sour. When things become hard, a lot of people find it very difficult to cope. And in order for them to deal with their pains and sorrows, some usually turn to narcotic substances that may help them forget, even if it's for a short time. When things got harder, more and more people began searching for these substances, which meant more customers for Delight and company who were very eager to provide and cash in. Money was made—a lot of it. Maromo, the main man on the ground, was now basking in glory. He had managed to expand the operations to cover many parts of Chitungwiza. The operations now spanned from St Mary's to most parts of Zengeza and Seke. Things were going so well that he had even managed to buy himself a car, a brand new Mazda B2200.

In their glory, the clique overlooked one crucial thing though, competition. The reality is: when it comes to anything that generates money, anything, whatever it is, be it legal or illegal, competition will always arise. As the months progressed, Maromo began to notice a slowdown in sales. This new development troubled him a lot. Why was the business slowing down? What was he doing wrong? He pondered. One weekend, whilst hanging out with one of his dealers, a young man called Yots, he casually asked why the business seemed to be slowing down. They were playing nine-ball pool that day at one of the pocket billiard tables around Chigovanyika, and like always, Maromo was losing heavily. He was already down by four games to one.

"It's because we aren't the only ones in the game anymore. There's a new guy who is supplying some good stuff," Yots said as he prepared to break. Maromo looked on in horror as the young man made a great hit. It was going to be a slaughter. Yots had managed to sink six balls, and on top of that, he still had clear control of the ball.

Maromo grimaced. "So where does this fella live?" he finally asked.

Yots remained silent for a short moment as he concentrated on the pool game, expertly sinking the 3 ball on the side pocket. This left him with only two balls: 8 and 9.

"Yots, I said where does this gentleman live?" Maromo asked again, quickly becoming irritated.

"He stays in Zengeza. I know the place," Yots said as he set himself up for 8 ball. He did not have any problems at all putting it away. A few moments later, he sank the 9 ball to win the game. Maromo shook his head and put his cue stick on the pool table. Sometimes he did not at all find any merriment in playing games with Yots. The lad won almost all the games, where was the fun in that? Maromo wondered, looking at Yots, who was now leaning on a nearby pole, smoking a joint.

"Are you going to pay for that?!" he snapped, angry because of the thrashing that he'd just received.

"Come on, *Mukoma*, have I ever let you down? Have I ever come up short?" Yots queried, dishing out an assuring grin.

Maromo glared at Yots. In that moment, there was nothing he would have wanted more than tying up the young man to a tree and whipping him thoroughly. "This supplier you are talking about, you said you know where he lives?" he finally asked.

"Yes, I do," Yots replied, nodding.

"Good," Maromo said as he scratched his head. "I need to have a talk with him, what he is doing is unacceptable."

"I wouldn't do that if I were you," Yots said, now looking nervous.

"Why?"

"The man is dangerous. He is not the kind you want to mess with." Maromo laughed loudly at this. "Take me to his house," he said.

Yots began to look visibly frightened. "I will, but please promise me that you will drop me off before we reach the house."

"If that's what you want."

As they were getting into the car Yots noticed that one of the car's headlights had been damaged. "When did that happen?" he asked.

"Last week. The kids smashed it whilst playing football. I will get it fixed soon."

It took them around ten minutes to reach their destination. The place looked deserted, Maromo noticed when he reached the entrance gate. If it were not for the music coming from the house, he would have concluded that no one lived there. A single glance was enough to tell you that the yard had not seen a broom for aeons. Two old broken-down cars parked in the front didn't help the scenery either. Even the hedge around the house was crying to be pruned. The only thing Maromo liked was the music. It was his favourite artist, Bob Marley, and the song being played was buffalo soldier.

Maromo knocked at the door, but no one answered. He knocked again for the second time, more loudly this time, but again, no one answered. He was about to return to his car when the door finally opened. When he turned to look, Maromo saw a dreadlocked fellow, who could be best described as a giant, now standing at the doorway. No wonder Yots had stayed behind, he thought. Hideous, with a face only a mother could love, the man before him was massive and terrifying. Maromo gulped.

"My man. How can I help you?" the dreadlocked gentleman inquired warmly.

Maromo considered his options. What could he possibly say to frighten this giant? He wondered. There were very few men who terrified him. When it came to the many streets fights he had been involved in, no man had yet managed to take him out. In that moment though, as he stood there face to face with the ugly giant, Maromo realised he had finally met his match. He needed to rethink his approach.

"Well, I was told that you have some good stuff," he winked. "You know, stuff to calm your nerves."

The fellow glared lengthily at him. Maromo froze. What was the man thinking? He wondered, already starting to feel uneasy.

"Who told you that?" the man demanded.

"A friend of mine."

"And who is this friend of yours?"

"You know what? I am sorry," Maromo quickly apologised. "Maybe I came to the wrong place," he said as he turned to leave.

"Wait! I just wanted to be sure that you are who you say you are. I think I might have something for you," the dreadlocked fellow finally said before disappearing into the house. He came back a few moments later with a small sachet which he handed to Maromo.

After paying for the sachet, Maromo immediately got into his car and drove off. Yots was waiting for him where he had left him.

"Did you talk to him?" Yots asked eagerly.

"I did," Maromo nodded.

"How did it go?"

"Huh?"

"I mean the conversation. How did it go? You saw the guy, he's terrifying, right?"

"Hey! Stop bugging me. I saw him, that's all you need to know."

Maromo responded angrily, fearing that if Yots continued asking questions, he would realise that he had been intimidated by the dreadlocked man.

Yots, surprised by the outburst, immediately became sullen and fell silent.

"I need to rush into town, where do you want me to drop you?" Maromo asked after they had driven for a few minutes in silence.

"Drop me at Huruyadzo."

Maromo nodded and increased his speed. After dropping Yots, he headed to the city.

When he arrived, he quickly searched for a payphone and called Delight.

"What is it, Maromo?" Delight answered. His voice sounded impatient.

"Boss. We have a problem."

"What kind of problem?"

"I have recently discovered that we now have a competitor."

"Really?! Come on, is that why you called me? Call me again when you have gotten rid of the bastard."

"That's the problem boss, I can't. You have to see this guy for yourself to understand what I am talking about. He's dangerous."

"Well, I hear you but I can't deal with this right now, is he that bigger of a threat?"

"Yes, he is. His stuff is quite good. Our sales have declined this past month, significantly."

For a moment, Delight remained silent. "Talk to Kam," he finally said. "Maybe he will come up with an idea. It's high time he tips in."

"Kam?" Maromo asked, surprised.

"Yes. Is there a problem?"

Maromo hesitated, "well, it's just that the man doesn't strike me as someone prepared to step over the line."

"Come on, give him a chance, will you. The man is already involved in the weed business. I think that counts as stepping over the line."

"Okay, boss. I will talk to him," Maromo said and hung up the phone.

As he walked out of the telephone booth onto the bustling street, Maromo felt unsure of what he was about to do. Would Kam really come up with any viable solution? Kam who had failed to handle the John situation? He looked at his wrist watch. It was now midday. At its highest point in the cloudless sky, the sun looked so bright and menacing, its blistering rays brilliantly brightening the modern buildings of Harare. Maromo walked casually from the telephone booth and got into his car. A few moments later, he arrived at Kam's shop. Kam was busy helping his employees to serve customers. When he saw Maromo, he immediately led him in to his office.

"So, what's up?" he asked when they had sat down.

"We have a problem, my friend," Maromo declared.

"So why did you come to me? I thought you were supposed to inform Delight if you encountered any hindrances?"

"I did. I talked to him, and he said that I should come to you."

Kam remained silent for a moment, pretending to organise the sheets of paper on his desk.

"So what happens to be the problem?" he finally asked.

"We now have a competitor, and he seems to be a formidable one. I think it's in our best interest if he is out of the picture."

Out of the picture? What did Maromo mean by that? Kam wondered. "Why don't we negotiate with him?" he suggested.

Maromo's expression became hard. "We are not going to cut anyone into our business," he said.

Kam remained silent for a moment. He didn't want blood on his hands again. Not after what he had gone through because of John's death. But then again, he also knew that this wasn't the moment to show weakness either. He had always complained that Maromo and Delight did many things behind his back. Having cold feet now when he'd finally been involved, he realised, would be a sign of undependability.

"Well, if that's the case why don't we rough him up a little? I think he will get the message."

Maromo thought about what Kam had said. He wasn't very convinced that the man's idea would work. For him, eliminating the dreadlocked guy was the best option. However, after a lengthy talk with Kam, he finally agreed to try out the idea. Who knew, he decided, maybe it would work. After his meeting with Kam, he drove back to Chitungwiza where he caught up with Yots again. The lad was in his usual spot at Huruyadzo, enjoying a Chibuku Scud whilst playing cards with a couple of other young fellas. Maromo got out of his car and approached them.

"*Munin'ina*, can I talk to you for a second," he said and took a sip from the Scud, which the group was drinking. Yots nodded and followed Maromo back to his car.

"Yots, my brother, can I count on you to do me a favour?"

"Of course, what do you want me to do?"

"Why don't we discuss it over a plate of *sadza*? I am starving, aren't you?"

Yots nodded and grinned. "I am, but I don't even have a coin on me though," he declared.

"How can you say you don't have money? Weren't you drinking a Scud just now?"

"I wasn't the one who was buying."

"Okay," Maromo said. "The food is on me."

He led Yots to a takeaway outlet nearby. The takeaway radiated a delightful aroma of cooked food. There, Maromo bought two plates of sadza and beef and then he and Yots proceeded to sit in an abandoned nearby shade to eat.

"So, what do you want me to help you with?" Yots asked after they had comfortably sat down.

"I want you to monitor the movements of that dreadlocked fella we visited earlier today."

"You mean Ras P?!"

"That's his name?" Maromo asked.

"You mean you still didn't know the man's name? Of course, that's his name."

"Good, I want you to observe his movements."

Yots vigorously shook his head. "You want me to monitor that monster?! I can't do that. If he discovers that's what I am doing, he'll have no trouble putting me down."

"Please, *Munin'ina*," Maromo pleaded. "Please, just do this for me. This once, and I promise I'll owe you big time."

"You are just saying that because you are a bit desperate right now. Why should I even believe you?"

"You know me. Yots, you know me. Have I ever let you down?"

Yots remained quiet for a moment. "Okay," he finally said after thinking for some time.

"Okay, I will do it."

Chapter 13

Someone once told me that poverty, in most instances, causes tension among people. When people lack the basic requirements for their subsistence, they end up becoming easily irate, and usually conflict is the end game. I am not sure how true this is, but I think this is what happened to Shorai and me. We ended up being two hungry people living in what I can honestly say an empty room. Caught up in the crisis of 98, when the prices of basic goods and rent rose rapidly, provoking widespread riots, we found ourselves among the multitude of the unfortunate victims. We were now struggling to pay rent and failing to afford most of our essential needs. Our business also started to go sour. We tried everything we could think of, but profits remained elusive. Instead of drawing closer in this trying time, we started quarrelling unnecessarily, blaming each other for the problems befalling us. We fought a lot, but for some time, we somehow managed to pull through. As the days went by, Shorai suddenly became distant, and at certain nights she would not sleep at home. I wasn't troubled much at first because she would always come up with convincing excuses every time I asked her where she'd spend the night, telling me she had spent the night at a female friend's house whilst sometimes she would proclaim having been at church for some all-night prayer.

However, Victor began giving me disturbing reports. He also advised me to monitor her movements. I did this, but no matter how I tried, I couldn't come up with the smoking gun. One morning, I woke up feeling an alien sensation around my genital area. I didn't think much of it, assuming that it would eventually go away. The feeling, however, actually became worse. As the day progressed, it was replaced by mild pain. I wondered what the cause of the pain could be, and several answers came into my head, none of which seemed convincing. I tried to ignore the pain and continued selling my wares, but the pain was not easy to ignore. It continued to increase its intensity, and by the time I returned home, I now felt as if an army of ants had invaded my whole genitalia. I confronted Shorai about this, but she stammered and became defensive, saying I had probably fooled around. This made me angry, and we ended up fighting. Shorai fled the room and disappeared into the night. Angry and in pain, I waited for her, thinking she would return in the course of the night, but she didn't come back.

The following day, I woke up and checked myself. I found out that my stick of joy had swollen, and something yellowish, with a very horrible smell, was now oozing from the tip. Shorai didn't come back that morning, and thinking she was at our store, I wobbled to the market later that day. It was not a pleasant experience at all, it was absolute torture, and the journey took me twice the time I used to take.

"What's wrong my friend? Are you feeling well?" Victor asked immediately after seeing me.

I shook my head. "No," I said. "Have you seen Shorai today?"

He shook his head, "I haven't seen her yet. Is there a problem?"

"Yes," I nodded. "I have a big problem right now. Let me show you something," I said, leading him to one of the market latrines. When I showed him what the 'problem' was, Victor leapt back, tripped and almost fell. It was as if he'd seen an enormous snake.

"Man!" he gasped. "You've been clapped."

He was confirming what I already knew. In the back of my mind, I had already known. I had refused to accept it, but I had known all along.

"Did Shorai do this to you?" he asked.

I nodded my head.

"Oh, man. This is so messed up."

"Do you know someone who sells legit stuff? A good herbalist who can fix me up?" I asked.

Victor thought for a while and then nodded, "there is someone who might help us."

"Really?!" I exclaimed, feeling a bit relieved.

"Yes," Victor said with a nod. "Let me take you to his house."

He immediately led me to the herbalist's home. When we reached the house, we found him sitting in his living room, watching TV. Victor did not waste time. He immediately explained the reason for our visit.

"Elder Doto," he said, addressing the herbalist, a dark complexed little man with a balding head. "We have come here to seek your help. My friend here has found himself in a very difficult situation."

"What's wrong with him?" Elder Doto inquired warmly.

Victor hesitated, "well, he has been clapped."

"Is that so?" Elder Doto said, looking at me.

I nodded.

"So when did you start noticing the symptoms?" he asked.

"Yesterday," I told him.

Elder Doto shook his head. "I am not surprised at all," he declared soberly. "Many young men are coming to my house a lot these days. I am going to tell you what I always tell each and every one of them. You boys need to be careful; you always have to protect yourselves these days….." He went on to say a lot of things, but I did not hear any of it. The pain I now felt in my genitalia had completely submerged even my sense of hearing. After the lecture, Elder Doto finally stood up from his seat and told us to follow him.

He led us to a small shed at the back of his house. The shed was full of different kinds of medicines: dried bulbs, bundles of herbs, roots and a lot of dried mushrooms. He selected an assortment of roots he wrapped in a newspaper and handed them to me, instructing me to boil the roots in water and then use it for cooking my porridge. After receiving the medicine, I immediately went back home feeling very hopeful that the medicine would work.

When I arrived at the house, I found out that Shorai had not yet come back. I was still angry with her, so I didn't even make an effort to find her. Instead, I proceeded to do what Elder Doto had instructed.

For the next two days I continued to do everything I had been instructed but things got worse. My joystick continued to swell. I couldn't sleep. The pain I felt was excruciating. My joystick began to look rotten, and I would cry every time I looked at it. By the third day, I could not take it anymore.

"I think you should just go to the clinic, my friend," Victor finally suggested when he came to see me that day.

"No! I can't do that," I told him. "Those health workers at the clinic will eat me alive."

Victor shrugged, "It can't be helped," he declared. "You will just have to brave it out."

"I can't go there, man," I continued resisting. "I just can't. I am too ashamed."

Victor patted my shoulder. "Look here, Tichakunda, this situation is already very bad. If you sit on this thing, it may actually become a lot worse than it is right now. If you insist you are that embarrassed, I will go with you then."

I thought about what Victor had said and realised that it made sense. The clinic was the only place I was assured of proper treatment, and at that moment, I urgently needed it.

Procrastinating would not get me anywhere. I eventually agreed to go.

When we finally reached the clinic, I felt as if I had walked for a very long distance. At the reception, I was greeted warmly by an elderly lady. She started asking me questions while writing the details on my health card.

"So what seems to be wrong, my son?" she finally asked gently. I wanted to reply, I did, but at that moment, words refused to come out of my mouth. Deeply confused and embarrassed with myself, I ended up just staring at her, grinning stupidly. The elderly lady looked at me, visibly disturbed by what I was doing. When she realised I was not going to talk, she finally stood up and looked at people behind me.

"Did anyone come with this young man?" she asked. Victor, who had been sitting at the end of the line, stood up and came forward.

"What's wrong with him?" she asked.

"He has been clapped."

"Clapped?"

"Yes, he has an STI."

"Oh, I see," she said, her expression immediately changing from that of empathy to that of a person who has just seen a pile of human excrement. She sighed and shook her head. "So that's why you were grinning like an imbecile? It was shame, wasn't it? Young people of these days; I seriously don't know what has gotten into you," she said as she finished scribbling on my hospital card. I felt so embarrassed, as if I'd been stripped of my clothes. When I turned to look at the people behind me, they were all staring at me, some with expressions of utter disgust on their faces. The elderly woman finally referred me to another office. When I entered it, I found a male nurse who had a no-nonsense attitude. He asked a lot of questions about my sex life.

After a period of intense questioning and tests, I was told I had contracted gonorrhoea. I was then given an injection and some antibiotic pills. The nurse also tested me for HIV. It was wise for me to know my status, he said before instructing me to sit on a bench outside, where I waited for my results. After a moment of anxious waiting, the nurse eventually called me back to his office. His face was vacuous, "Mr Bungira, your results came back positive."

"Positive?" I leapt off my chair, my hands on my head. I knew what a positive result meant. I had learnt about it at school. I started pacing up and down the room, thinking.

"Why don't you sit down and relax, Mr Bungira?" the nurse advised.

I sat down and started crying. I could not believe what I had just heard. The nurse, however, eventually managed to calm me down.

Things weren't as bad as I thought, he said. Being positive was not the end of the world. I still had a long life ahead of me. People like me could continue living long, healthy lives if they adopted a positive lifestyle. He went on to tell me that he had admitted me into a health club that consisted of people who were also positive like me.

The club had been created so that people like me would help each other deal with the problems they faced in their daily lives. He gave me the addresses of some of the people who were in the club. Visit them anytime you can. It can help, he advised. After the whole treatment and counselling process, I felt exhausted. I collected my medication and headed straight home.

I was so angry at that moment. I thought about Shorai. Where was she right now? Did she even know that she was positive? The whole situation was proving to be too much for me. As I headed back, I decided I would make her give me money for bus fare. Early the next morning, I would go back home. These plans, however, went through the window when I reached the house. Our room was now empty. All the things were gone. The only things I found were a couple of cockroaches loitering around. I was dumbstruck, I was absolutely staggered. In a state of utter disorientation, I knocked on Tindo's door. "Have you seen what happened to our things?" I asked.

Tindo nodded. "Yes, Shorai took them. She left a few minutes ago. She told me that you had both decided to relocate."

I could not believe what I was hearing. My legs felt weak, and I immediately sat down on the floor. Tindo stared at me, her face now looking remorseful.

"Do you have any idea where she might have gone?" I asked her, my voice cracking. Tindo shook her head. At that moment, the situation I was in slowly began to dawn on me. I felt tears welling up and seeping out of my eyes. Victor, who had accompanied me, quickly knelt beside me. "Do not strain yourself with this," he said. "What has been done has already been done. I don't think there is anything you can do about this. Look on the bright side. You still have two more weeks before you will be required to pay the rent again."

"Is that supposed to make me feel better?" I asked, "where am I supposed to find money to go back home now?"

Victor remained silent for a moment. "There is someone who I can hook you up with for quick money if you are bold."

"Quick money?"

"Yes," he said, pulling me out of the house. "There is this brother who can supply you with stuff to sell. He will give you 20 percent of the dough you make. Believe me, it's a lot of money."

"What are you talking about? I don't understand."

Victor reached into his pockets and pulled out a small sachet with dried leaves in it. "You sell *mbanje*?!" I blurted out in surprise.

"Shhhh, lower your voice. Remember, you don't need to do this for long. You just need to do it for a few days, then you'll be done."

I thought about it for a moment. "So, where can I meet this guy?" I finally asked.

"Come to the market tomorrow, I'm sure he'll drop by. I'll introduce you to him," he said.

That night, the other tenants, after hearing what had happened, felt pity for me and came to my rescue. Tindo gave me two of her very old pots that she wasn't using anymore, and the other tenant, the bus rank tout, some mealie meal and a bundle of vegetables. Victor's mother too, hearing what had happened, offered me a tattered blanket and an old paraffin stove. I gladly accepted the things. I was nothing but grateful. That whole night I remained awake, thinking about Victor's proposal, about my life. The desire to continue living in the city had now completely deserted me. I now wanted to go home. Unable to come up with another way to make money for the bus fare, I finally decided to sell the drugs for a few days.

The following day, thinking that I might run into her, I passed through the spot where Shorai and I had used to sell our wares, but she wasn't there. I then proceeded to Victor's store, where I helped him serve his customers as I waited for the man he'd told me about.

At around 3 pm, a white Mazda B2200 finally pulled beside the store. A heavily built gentleman emerged from the car. Victor smiled and patted me on the back.

"Tichakunda, this is bro Maromo," he said. "This is the guy I have been telling you about."

Chapter 14

It had been almost three weeks since Kam had met with Maromo. After that meeting, he had not seen him again, and he was now getting anxious. What was Maromo up to? Had he already solved the problem of the other supplier yet? Kam wondered. Maybe it was high time he visited the man at his home, he thought. Since the day he had gone there after his return from Gondola, Kam had never forgotten the house. Although he had arrived there at night, he was sure he would remember the way.

When he reached the house in St Mary's, Kam was relieved to see Maromo's white Mazda B2200 parked outside. He pressed the horn button, and shortly after, Maromo emerged.

"Mr Kam, what a pleasant surprise," Maromo exclaimed as he approached the car. "What brings you here?" he asked.

"Well, it's been three weeks so I thought I should come and see how things are going."

"Oh, don't worry yourself. I've got a man working on it. He's still monitoring the situation. When something more promising comes up, I'll fill you in," Maromo reassured.

"Are you sure?"

"Definitely."

"So, how are your kids doing? How is your wife?"

Maromo smiled weakly and shrugged.

"What's wrong?" Kam asked.

Maromo laughed. "What do you want me to say, it's a marriage. You will understand when you get married."

"I need to be married to understand?"

"I think you do. Do you have someone?"

"Yes, I do."

"Does she know?" Maromo asked.

"Know what?"

"About your extracurricular activities."

"What! No, she doesn't, and it will remain that way."

"Are you sure?" Maromo queried. "A secret is like a seed buried in the soil you know, all it needs is a bit of moisture for it to geminate. Have you ever asked yourself what would happen if she were to find out?"

Kam shook his head. "That is not going to happen," he insisted.

Maromo shrugged, "whatever you say, my man."

As he drove back to his house, Kam began to think about what Maromo had said. Although he had insisted that Susan would never find out, he knew that Maromo's fears were spot on. He wasn't much worried about Susan though, from the time they had begun their relationship, she had never been inquisitive. It was her mother he was concerned about. Tanya was one of those people who were proverbially curious.

About a week after his trip to Chitungwiza, Kam was sitting in his office going through the accounts books when Maromo walked in.

"Everything is now in place. It's on today," he declared.

"Today?" Kam asked, a bit surprised.

"Yes, today. I have been assured that the man would likely be alone at his house tonight."

"So we'll stick to the original plan?"

"Yes. We'll just knock at his door. He'll come out. He won't even suspect a thing."

"Are you sure?" Kam queried.

"Absolutely."

Kam didn't argue. Maromo seemed sure of himself. At lunch, Kam went back home and changed his clothes. He also notified his mother that he would be coming back home late that day. There was a business venture he was planning with some friends. At around eleven PM, he drove to Chitungwiza. When he arrived at Maromo's house, Kam found him already standing at the gate with another young man whom he introduced as Yots. As time was of the essence, Kam got into Maromo's car, and the three men immediately drove to Ras P's house. The place was very quiet. Save for the lights, one would have thought that no one was at home. Maromo knocked and waited. After a few moments, they heard some movement inside. A short moment later, Ras P opened the door and stood in the doorway. Kam took a step back, surprised by what he saw. When Maromo had told him that the man was intimidating, Kam had not taken it seriously. The man was indeed gargantuan; he was massive. If there were payphones nearby, he would have gladly called the Guinee's Book of Records. He began to wonder if their plan was going to work. What could they possibly do to intimidate this giant? He wondered.

"Can I help you, gentleman?" Ras P asked.

"Yes. You can do that by immediately stopping your drug operations. This is our territory," Maromo said, drawing a pistol and pointing it at Ras P.

"Really? Says who?" Ras P asked, looking at the gun. He did not seem to be bothered by it at all.

"Me," Maromo replied. "Don't even think of doing anything stupid. We know your family, and we know where you live. If you refuse to stop, you and your loved ones will pay," Maromo icily declared.

Ras P burst out laughing. It was a nerve-wracking laugh.

"So you three cockroaches had the nerve to come here with some cheap toy gun, and you thought what, you could intimidate me?" Ras P asked, stepping forward, his voice now a little horse with anger. "You are very lucky to have found me in a happy mood. I'm going to do something I've never done before; I am going to give you three gentlemen a chance to walk away. So please, gentlemen, please, just walk away."

"I am sorry, my friend, but we cannot do that," Maromo said.

Ras P shrugged his shoulders and spit on the ground, "Well, I guess what we have reached here is called an impasse. So, tell me, what are you going to do about it?"

Maromo made a step forward, his gun still pointed at Ras P, "my friend, trust me on this one, trust me. You really don't want to mess with us."

Ras P remained quiet for a moment. "Do you have any idea how many people sell weed around here?" he finally asked.

Maromo remained silent.

"We don't have to kill each other over this," Ras P said. "Many people sell drugs in this neighbourhood. Some sell pills, others intoxicating cough syrups. We are all struggling, we are all trying to get by."

"I don't care about what you are saying. Are you going to stop selling your weed or not?" Maromo demanded.

Ras P began laughing again. "Okay, I think we are done here. Now get the hell off my yard!" he said, advancing towards Maromo.

"Stop there, or I will shoot!" Maromo warned.

"Really?" Ras P sneered, "we will see about that," he said, taking another step forward.

"Stop right there. I'm warning you. If you move again, I'll shoot, that's a promise," Maromo hissed.

By now, Kam and Yots had retreated to a safe distance. Damn those cowards, Maromo swore silently. At this moment, Ras P had transitorily stopped. Maromo glared at the man. He did not like what he saw. The man did not seem to be scared at all, instead, he looked mad. Maromo regarded his options. If Ras P somehow managed to grab him or get hold of him, he had no doubt that this would be his end. But how was he going to convince this man to stop his operations? Maromo wondered. He could not shoot Ras P. This would only attract unnecessary attention. Using this pistol to do that would again probably not be a good idea. He had used it somewhere else before. As Maromo pondered, Ras P launched at him. Startled by this sudden advance, he accidentally pressed the trigger. The pistol spat a projectile which hit Ras P squarely in the chest. This, though, did not stop Ras P from moving towards Maromo, it merely slowed him down. Maromo immediately realised the desperate situation he was now in. He knew he could not expect any help from his companions. He had noticed them scrambling for the car like two little chicks running from an eagle when he fired the shot. He raised his pistol and aimed for the head. He did not miss. Like a tall tree that has been severely chopped up, Ras P fell heavily to the ground. Maromo turned and ran back to the car. Kam and Yots were already inside. The moment Maromo got in, Kam stepped hard on the accelerator, and the car quickly sped off.

"Why did you do that?" Kam frantically asked when they had driven to a safe distance.

"I didn't have a choice," Maromo said with intense desperation. "If that man had grabbed me, I would've been a corpse by now. It was either him or me. I chose me." Kam and Yots looked at each other and remained quiet.

"Do you think anyone saw our car?" Maromo asked, looking very worried.

"I don't think so," Kam replied. "I was on the lookout all the time. I didn't see anyone."

"If someone did see us, well, then we are done," Yots remarked dryly.

. . . . . .

Ten days later. Some kilometres from Ras P's house, in the capital city, specifically in an office within the criminal investigation department at the general police headquarters, Chief Superintendent Chimusuwa was sitting in his office browsing through the latest Herald newspaper. There was a knock on his door. He told the person to enter, and a young lad from the Forensic Science Unit walked in.

"So, what's the news, officer?" Chief Superintendent Chimusuwa asked.

"It's about that shooting in Zengeza, ten days ago, sir," the young officer replied.

"Did you find anything that may be of help to the investigation?"

"Yes, we did, sir. After analysing the gun cartridges found at the crime scene, we discovered that the gun is the same as the one used in a murder case that had gone cold, which happened five years ago at the Masawu Flats where a man was shot and killed in his room."

"Now that's interesting," Chief Superintendent Chimusuwa remarked, rubbing his chin. "Is that all?"

"Yes sir," the young officer nodded.

"Okay then. You are excused officer."

The young officer saluted and left. Chimusuwa immediately dialled St Mary's police station. "Hello, this is Chief Inspector Tsvubvu speaking," a voice boomed from Chimusuwa's receiver." Tsvubvu was the officer in charge of the St Mary's police station.

"Tsvubvu, it's me, it's Chimusuwa. Some new intel has emerged regarding that Zengeza murder case. The gun that was used to shoot that fella was also used five years ago in another case in Mbare. You should link up with the guys at Mbare Police station to see if you can share information. I think you should work together to solve this one."

"But *Shefu*…"

"Tsvubvu. That's an order.

"Ok *Shefu*, I will get on it immediately."

"Good," Chief Superintendent Chimusuwa said. "Put your best guys from CID Homicide on it immediately. We need to urgently catch this criminal."

Chapter 15

When I met Maromo for the first time, he had looked at me in an unusual way, visibly unsettled by my presence. I was greatly alarmed by this. I could not understand why a terrifying man like him could be made anxious by someone like me. Had we ever met before? He'd asked. No, I shook my head. We had certainly never met before. Are you sure? He kept asking. Yes, I am sure, I told him. Well, maybe his eyes were playing tricks with him. Maybe he had met someone who looked like me, he wasn't sure. Maromo was our boss. He supplied us the weed and advised us on the prices to charge. For our efforts, we retained twenty percent of the money we made.

When I started selling weed, the original plan was to do it for a few days, get some money, and then go back home. But as the days progressed, I began to ponder. What would I do back home? How would I survive? Had Aunt and her husband returned? If they had, what would they think of me after all that had happened? What about the people in our village, how would they react when they saw me? People judge; people talk. Not yet prepared to deal with the criticism which I was likely to receive back home, I finally decided to stay. I was now making a lot of money from the weed I was selling. I was discovering a lot of interesting things too. When I started, I thought that I would be selling the drug to young unemployed adults who were depressed and had nothing to do. As it turned out, the habit did not discriminate. It could affect anyone, be it the rich or the poor, the young or the elderly.

My customers came in the form of teachers, executives and sometimes even pastors.

Besides selling it, I had also started smoking the weed. I had decided to try it one day and had discovered that it made you feel good and relaxed. The downside was that you ended up wanting more of it. To ensure that I wouldn't use up my stash and end up in trouble with my boss, I had to use other drugs as well. Victor had introduced me to a cough syrup called Broncleer. In the streets we called it *Bronco*. I usually took it when I was thinking too much about my situation and couldn't sleep. I always kept a bottle, the drug sent me into a deep sleep every time I took it. However, you have to have money to buy the broncleer, so during periods we ran out of money, we had to improvise. Someone had come up with an idea of mixing the white residue found in used pampers with water and boiling it. When boiled, the mixture turned into a greyish semi-solid which we then drank. The greyish stuff smelled and tasted awful, but since we wanted to get high, we took it anyway. The thing is, during those short moments after we took it, we would temporarily forget everything: all our problems, our fears, and our sorrows. The problems didn't go away of course, after getting sober they would still be there, staring at us right in the face. This meant that we had to take the drugs again to make us forget. That's just how it works, it's a vicious cycle. There's no running away from it. In the end, we could not function normally without taking the drugs. We literally became slaves to the habit.

I knew what I was doing was wrong, but I couldn't bring myself to stop using the drugs. They became part of my life, once I got hooked, it wasn't easy to walk away.

I continued living in the same room in which I had lived with Shorai, despite the bad memories it brought. I had to; it was quite affordable, not to mention convenient because of its closeness to the market. I also didn't relocate because it is very hard to find accommodation in Harare, especially for people who are relatively new to the city. I had also decided to do vending again to cover my 'tracks'. I had been given this idea by Victor, who was now sort of a mentor. He was the one who taught me the rules of the game. The primary rule was never to get caught because if you were caught, well, then you were on your own. Blabbermouths were not tolerated. If you informed on anyone, you could pay dearly, and sometimes with your life. The other most important rule was to respect boundaries. Each dealer had his spot along the roads which went through Mbare, where customers knew that they could find us. Failure to respect boundaries by invading the selling spots of other dealers could prove costly. If you disregarded the boundaries, the others could end up giving you heavy makeup. There was one guy I knew who had ended up losing all his front teeth because of this.

I had not made any effort to get in touch with the other members of my health group. Not sure if entering the group meant that you had to be open about your status, I shunned it. When it came to my status, I was not yet ready to be open about it. Most people I met believed that being positive meant that you would have already kicked the bucket. You would always be shunned. Some people, ignorant about the disease, could even refuse to share a toilet facility with you. There was a general view that all those infected were immoral people who were so vile and deprecating to society. So although I had been very shocked at first, I had decided to deal with my status on my own. I ultimately thought I would be okay. As someone who had gone to school, I never thought that I would have problems accepting and handling it. Being young, I still had the naivety and arrogance of thinking that I could handle anything on my own.

As days passed, I became bitter. I began to find it increasingly hard to handle Shorai's betrayal and come to terms with what she had done to me. In an attempt to ease the pain, I would always find myself using drugs, or in a bar with Victor, drinking intemperately, but it didn't end my pain. The next morning I would always wake up sober, remembering. In those days, I found myself at the loneliest point of my life. If you ask those who have ever reached this point, they will tell you that it's like drowning in a chilly pool. It's like being buried under an enormous blanket of very cold water, a very painful, traumatising and suffocating experience.

One afternoon, walking home after having had a drink or two to drown my sorrows, I ran into the nurse who had tested me. It was so sudden, so sudden that I was not able to avoid him. He was with his wife and child, going in the direction of the market.

"Hi, I know you. You are Tichakunda, right?" he said immediately after seeing me.

"Yes, I am. How are you, nurse?" I replied, trying the best I could to hide my drunken face.

"You are drunk, aren't you, Tichakunda?"

"Oh no, not at all," I lied.

"So, how are you coping?" he said with some concern in his voice.

"I am okay," I told him. "Actually, I have never been this okay all my life."

The nurse shook his head. "You are not okay," he said, looking at me and then at his wife, who had walked ahead. She was now standing beside the road, looking very impatient. "You know what," he said. "Why don't you come to the clinic tomorrow? We really need to talk."

"I will see what I can do," I told him. He nodded, patted my shoulder and started walking towards his family, leaving me to continue my journey home. Seeing him had not helped matters at all. It was like going back to that day I had been tested. That day my life had forever changed. Suddenly I was feeling depressed again. When I reached home, I cooked dinner, but I did not eat anything at all. I lay down and began thinking about what I was going to do in the next few days. Christmas was upon us, and the year 98 was now drawing to an end. What was I going to do on Christmas day? I pondered. I wasn't going to spend it loitering around with Victor, that's for sure. He had big plans, and he was in high spirits. His crush, whom he had been chasing for quite some time, had finally relented, and he was looking forward to spending the whole festive day with her.

I brooded for a while, thinking that I would eventually fall asleep, but this did not happen. Looking at my watch later, I saw that the time was already approaching midnight. It didn't look like I was going to enter the dominion of night visions any time soon by the air of things. I didn't have a bottle of broncleer around so I immediately got up and headed for the bar. Maybe a pint or two of beer would knock me out.

I had just walked a couple of hundred metres from my house when I saw her, one of the local streetwalkers. I knew her; I had seen her at one of the bars the other day when Victor and I were having some drinks. When I saw her, I was quickly struck by her dressing; a black top and tight fitting red miniskirt that left her gleaming thighs exposed. I approached her and asked if she would be okay coming back with me to my house. She smiled and readily agreed. As I was about to go into my room, Tindo walked out of her room, possibly heading for the bathroom. When she saw the lady and me behind, her eyes grew as wide as those of an owl. She had an expression of disapproval on her face, but I ignored her and entered my room.

The next day I woke up feeling a little light-headed. I did not feel like waking up. I had finally decided what I was going to do during the Christmas holiday. I had decided to spend the day selling my weed. On Christmas, people would be having fun. They would be wild and needing product. This was the time to make that dough, and I wasn't going to let the chance just slip away.

I was making some tea to help me with my hangover when I heard a knock on the door. When I opened it, I found Tindo outside. Her face looked solemn. "Can I come in?" she said.

I hesitated for a moment.

"Of course," I finally said and stepped aside to let her in.

This was her first time coming into my room since Shorai had left. She stood in the middle of the room and looked around. Why was she here? What did she want? I wondered.

"I notice you are now bringing in friends," she said.

An image of our awkward encounter in the corridor last night flashed through my mind. I grinned and looked on the floor.

"I know this might be embarrassing to you, and annoying, me prying into your private life like this, but you have to understand that I am a mother. It's in my nature to want to help."

"I am ok," I said.

"Are you sure? From the way you have been behaving these past days, you seem lonely," she said.

I remained quiet.

Tindo sighed and shook her head. "Have you made an effort to find where Shorai is?" she asked.

"Why would I? She left me," I said.

Tindo looked at me for a while in silence. "Why do you sound like it's all her fault?" she said

"It is. She abandoned me," I said bitterly.

"But she just didn't leave? Did she Tichakunda? She left because you hit her."

"We fought," I said.

Tindo shook her head. "That's not what she told me," she said. "You know where she is?"

"I do. She reached out. If you want to see her I will tell you where she is if you promise me there will be no violence," she said.

I remained silent for a while and then shook my head. "No," I finally said. "I don't want to see her."

Later that morning, as I was leaving the house for some meetings with a few customers, I saw a group of people coming in to the front yard. I instantly knew who they were the moment I laid my eyes on them. Stupid me. At that moment, I realised I had completely forgotten about the appointment I'd made with the nurse the previous day. I was without doubt that he was the one who had sent them. They were five of them, a man in his thirties, three middle-aged women and a girl of my age.

"Hi Mr Bungira, we are from the Aids Support Group," the man greeted me.

"Hi," I replied nervously.

"Mr Kunatsa sent us here. He thought that you might want our help."

"Mr Kunatsa?"

"Yes, the nurse from the clinic."

"Oh, I see," I nodded.

"Could we come in?" he asked.

I thought for a moment, then finally decided that there was no harm in letting them in.

"My name is Nhengeni," the man said once we had settled. "Mr Kunatsa said that you might have some questions concerning our group, so he advised us to visit you so that we could put everything into clear perspective, but let me introduce the others first. This lady sitting here is mother Gombwe," the man said, pointing to the lady who was seated to his right.

"This is mother Kureba," he said, referring to the woman who was seated to his left.

"The woman sitting close to you is mother Chireshe, and the young lady there is Natsai."

"I am honoured to meet you all," I said. "Thank you for coming to see me."

"So, is it true that you had some questions?"

"Well, I had some concerns. I especially wanted to know if joining your group meant that one had to openly disclose their status to the public," I said.

Mother Kureba shook her head, "that's a personal decision. It's not a requirement to enter the group. We are just here to help each other deal with trauma and everyday difficulties that people who are positive face."

"So you can still keep your status secret?" I asked.

"Of course," Mother Chireshe concurred.

I nodded while closely looking at everyone in the room. They all looked healthy. Their skin sparkled. Were they all positive? I wondered.

"So you being here, does that mean you are all positive?" I asked.

"Yes," the girl, Natsai replied. "We are all positive. That's why we came up with the idea of forming the group. We did it so that we could help each other. I think it will be good for you if you could join. Will you consider joining us now that all your fears have been allayed?" Natsai asked courteously.

"Since you have made everything clear to me, I think I will," I said, smiling and feeling reassured. I wasn't lying. I had finally decided to join the club, and I wasn't only joining to get help. I was also doing this because of the girl. For some reason I couldn't fathom, she had stirred some strong emotions within me, emotions which I couldn't suppress.

Chapter 16

After the incident in Zengeza, Kam spent the following days pregnant with fear. Had anyone seen them or their car? He wondered. Were they in any way under some suspicion? What would happen if they got caught? Of the three, he was the most fearful. He found himself always trembling. About a week after the incident, he caught a fever and became violently sick. He had to remain in bed for a couple of days. Maromo, too, was anxious during this time; but not enough to stop business. He maintained his routine, behaving as if nothing had happened. He had been through something like this before. When it happened the first time, he had been very scared, thinking something would happen to him, but nothing had happened. If nothing had happened then, he reasoned, well, nothing was likely to happen now. Besides, Kam had assured him that no one had seen them that night, so there was nothing to worry about. Business was booming again, and he had recruited more people. It wasn't hard to find foot soldiers. There were lots of young men and women loitering. Most of them literally jumped at the chance to sell the drugs.

Maromo had, however, been unnerved by one of his recruits. A young man from Mbare. The face of the young man had made the hairs on his back stand up. Why this was so, Maromo wasn't sure. He was sure that he had met the young man somewhere though. Where? He wasn't sure. If the boy hadn't seemed so desperate, Maromo would surely not have recruited him. There was one more thing that was troubling him. Maromo had not yet told Delight about the killing. He wasn't sure how his boss would react. He certainly knew that Kam would have said nothing. The man was a coward and probably in bed now, frightened and shitting his pants. How about

Yots? Maromo wondered. He hadn't seen the young man since the incident. He was now concerned about him. Had the incident become too much for the young man? Highly unlikely. Yots had been through a lot. The young man had been an illegal gold miner once, and there in the mine shafts, he had seen a lot of violence and witnessed lives being lost. However, Maromo could not settle for assumptions, he decided to visit the young man to see how he was faring.

He got into his B2200 and headed to Yots' house. When he arrived there, he found Yots' wife outside, washing clothes. Maromo frowned when he saw her; love is undeniably blind. It is an enigmatic emotion that is truly arduous to comprehend. Yots' wife was a relic. The woman was old enough to be the young man's Grandmother. Whatever Yots saw in her, Maromo couldn't understand. What is it you see in this woman? Maromo would always ask. Yots would smile broadly, his eyes sparkling. "Oh, you don't know sweet mama as I do; she is lit. She's the best," he would say. Unable to comprehend the whole thing, Maromo would sometimes be left wondering just how good sweet mama was. However, one thing was clear: the young man's heart belonged to sweet mama, to her and her alone.

"Is Yots around?" Maromo asked as he approached Yots' wife.

"Yes, he is," she nodded. "He's inside, sleeping."

Of course, he is, Maromo thought.

Yots' wife went inside the house and came back a few moments later, with Yots closely following behind her.

"*Mukoma*," Yots smiled, his face still looking sleepy. "What brings you here?"

"I haven't seen you in a while," Maromo responded. "I had to check up on you."

"Thanks for the concern, but I am fine."

"I can see that," Maromo concurred.

Yots leaned and whispered in Maromo's ear, "besides," he said. "Sweet mama is taking good care of me."

"I noticed that too," Maromo remarked dryly.

Yots laughed. "So, is everything okay on your side?" he asked.

"Never better. It's actually you I was starting to worry about. I couldn't find you in all your favourite spots."

"I decided to stay low for a while. I thought it was for the best."

"Well, I see your point of view, but we must not behave as if we are anxious about something. I want you to go back and do what you've always been doing. Okay?"

"Alright *Mukoma*, I understand. So is Mr Kam alright? How is he doing?"

"I am not sure. Last time I checked him at his shop, his employees told me that he was still sick."

Yots laughed. "We have to be careful about that one. Do you think he can handle this?"

"I don't know," Maromo said. "I just don't know."

"Maybe you should check on him again," Yots suggested.

"That's a good idea," Maromo agreed.

Immediately after his chat with Yots, Maromo headed to town, reaching Kam's shop about half an hour later. He went inside acting like an ordinary customer. Kam's mother would be around sometimes, and he did not want to make her suspicious. When he entered the shop though, he realised that she wasn't around.

"Is your boss in?" he asked one of Kam's employees, TK, whom he usually conversed with every time he visited the shop. TK nodded and pointed towards Kam's office. Maromo did not waste time. He went into the little office where he found Kam sitting in his chair, looking very sullen. There was a cup of tea on his table, which stood there untouched.

Maromo picked up the cup and drained its contents into his mouth.

"What are you doing?!" Kam exclaimed in agitation.

Maromo shrugged. "The tea was already cold, and you clearly didn't want it. So, what's the big deal?"

"That's your excuse for drinking my tea without asking?"

"Ok. Maybe I shouldn't have done that, I am so sorry. Now is not the time to argue at all. We need to talk. Have you told Delight about the incident yet?"

Kam shook his head, "No, I didn't. Besides, you know I was sick at home. I thought you told him."

"I didn't. You know the man. He's not very fond of screw-ups."

"So, what should we do?" Kam asked.

"I really don't know. I have run out of ideas."

"Maybe we should just call him. We eliminated a rival, so I don't think he'll be mad. On the contrary, I think he'll be elated."

"Of course, he'll be elated that the man is no more. That's not what I'm worried about."

"It's not that? What's the problem then?" Kam asked.

Maromo hesitated. "It's about the gun."

"What about it?" Kam queried.

"Well, it's the same gun that was used on John."

For a moment, Kam glared at Maromo, his lips quivering. "You son of a bitch!" he finally yelled, grabbing Maromo's collar. "So it's been you this whole time?"

"I can explain," Maromo said as he tried to loosen himself from Kam's hold. As he was frantically trying to free himself from the grip, he received a shove that left him and the chair he was sitting on crushing on the ground.

"Is everything okay in here?" TK, who had heard the noise, asked as he peeped through the door.

"It's okay," Kam responded. "Go back to work," he said as he dialled on his phone.

"Wait! What are you doing?" Maromo exclaimed as he scrambled from the floor.

"I am calling Delight."

"But we haven't decided what we are going to say to him yet."

"We? There is no we. You shot the man, so this is your problem."

"Please, let's..."

"Hello," Delight's voice boomed from the receiver cutting Maromo's pleas prematurely.

"Hi Delight, It's me. It's Kam."

"Oh, it's you. Hi my friend. How are you? Why have you been so silent lately?" Delight asked.

"I was sick," Kam said.

"You have now fully recovered, I hope?"

"Yes, I have."

"That's good to hear," Delight declared. "So, how is the business doing?"

"Oh, things couldn't be better. We got rid of that competitor."

"You got rid of him?"

"Yes."

"That's good news. How?"

"Maromo shot him," Kam said with a wide grin to the objection of Maromo. Delight remained quiet for a moment. "Maromo shot him?" he finally asked.

"Yes."

"Have you seen him lately?" Delight inquired.

"He is actually here," Kam said as he handed the phone to Maromo, who was frantically waving his hands to signal him to stop. Maromo was terrified of Delight. The man was the only boss he had ever known. Maromo had met Delight in South Africa. He had been an illegal migrant back then, a young man who was trying to make a living in a foreign country. Things had not turned out as he had planned, so he had ended up on the streets. This is where his boss had discovered him. It was Delight who had taught Maromo everything he knew about the drug trade.

Maromo received the phone from Kam, his hands shaking.

"Hi b-boss," he stammered into the phone.

"Please tell me you did not use that pistol which I clearly told you to get rid of?" Delight demanded. Maromo did not say anything, he remained quiet.

"Damn it!" Delight cursed. "Do you have any idea of what you have done? You retard!" he thundered.

Maromo frightened, shrunk into his chair. "I did not mean to kill the man boss. It's just that he did not give me a choice. If he had co-operated, this would never have happened," he reasoned.

"Shut your stinking mouth!" Delight hissed. "You are responsible for this mess. I told you to get rid of that gun a long time ago."

"I didn't have any choice, boss. The man was about to attack me," Maromo fearfully insisted.

"Well, let's hope that the cops will not connect the dots. I have a man inside. I'll talk to him. He will keep me informed about the investigation," Delight said and hung up.

Maromo laid down the phone looking at Kam, who was wearing a smug smile and walked out of the office. Although he did not like what Kam had done, he did not fret. It was Kam's moment. Sooner or later, he knew he would also have his. When he left Kam's shop, he drove back to Chitungwiza. Halfway through the journey, he decided to visit Chikwanha, a small township located just outside Chitungwiza. The small township can be best described as a place of little restraint. A lot of street walkers can be found there. It's a small township with many vendors, a few takeaways, several bars and nightclubs; it's a place where the wild and adventurous can be found—those who are not afraid to pursue their weirdest and unspeakable desires. Maromo being one of those people, decided to drop in. He wanted to forget his troubles for the moment. At the township, he found himself in one of the nightclubs. It did not take him long to find a sporting lady who wanted to have fun. With a few takeaways, some weed and a few bottles of booze, he and his lady friend ended up engaging in the rites of libertinage in a nearby lodge. At around 11 pm, drunk and spent, he finally headed home, home to his wife and kids. When he reached the house, he found the whole family already asleep. His wife was already in bed, snoring herself out. Seeing this, Maromo thanked the heavens, the angels and God All Mighty too. He could go straight to sleep. There would be no interrogation today. He got into his pyjamas and silently tucked himself into bed, making sure not to wake his wife up.

"Where the hell have you been?" his wife's voice suddenly boomed.

Maromo almost had a heart attack. Really? All this time she had been awake? All this time?! She couldn't be serious. So she had deliberately given him false hope.

"Sweetheart, hi, I didn't mean to wake you up," Maromo said, trying the best he could to sound quixotic.

"Didn't you hear what I said, you sick bastard? I said, where the hell have you been?!"

"Look, honey, I don't want to fight with you, okay? Why don't we just sleep? Let's talk about this tomorrow."

Maromo's wife rose to a sitting position, "I said where were you?!" she thundered.

"You know very well where I was. You know my work, there were things I was taking care of," Maromo said.

"Oh really? You take me for an idiot, don't you? I know that you were at Chikwanha with some prostitute today. My friend saw you there."

Maromo immediately became meek. Stupid him. How could he forget that some of his wife's friends worked at Chikwanha? He had made a terrible blunder. What in the world was he going to say now?

His wife let out a very deep sigh. "You know what? You are right. Between us, no one wants to fight. So why don't you take a spare blanket and go make yourself comfortable on the sofa."

"Oh, come on," Maromo moaned. "If you make me do that, I will go straight to file for a divorce tomorrow morning."

Maromo's wife let out a very loud and sarcastic laugh. "No, you won't," she said. "In case you forgot, I own you."

Maromo covered his head with sheets and closed his eyes. Better to ignore this woman. He wasn't going to win the argument anyway, so what was the purpose of having it then? He was about to enter into the magnificent realm of dreams when he heard a farting sound. The sleep he so much wanted immediately slipped from his grasp. Maromo scrambled for the sheets and covered his nose. He quickly turned to look at his wife, but she snored away as if nothing had happened. Maromo stumbled out of bed, humbled. He knew this was a fight he would never win; he could never come up with something smellier, even if he tried. Besides, he was not in the mood for fighting. He was tired. He needed to rest. Shaking his head, he took a spare blanket and headed towards the sitting room, where he tried, without success, to make himself comfortable on the sofa.

Chapter 17

Chief Inspector Tsvubvu was a man of moody disposition. He was very short. His colleagues called him *chigusvani*, although none of them dared to say this in his presence. He liked to quarrel a lot and was rather difficult to get along with. Due to a car accident two years before, he walked with a limp, something which he was very bitter about. He had a tendency to question orders from his superiors but when he took on a task, he was ruthlessly immediate and effective, traits which had led to his rapid promotion within the police force.

After receiving the call from his superior, Chief Inspector Tsvubvu realised that there would be a lot of work in the following days. The Zengeza case had left him bowled over. At the moment, the police did not have any main suspects. Something like this had never happened before. It was very rare that someone could be shot in Zengeza without anyone witnessing the incident. Why had the man been shot? Was the perpetrator going to strike again? He wondered. He was in a bad mood. What his superior had ordered him to do exasperated him. He felt his station didn't need to actively involve Mbare police station in order to solve the case. He sat thinking about the case for a while and then stood from his desk and walked into the next office.

"Sergeant, who is the commanding officer at Mbare police station?" he asked. The Sergeant looked blankly back at him.

Chief Inspector Tsvubvu limped out. "Never mind," he said. "Let me head there."

He took the Land rover defender and drove to Mbare police station. It was his first visit to the station. Some of the station's constables were standing outside chatting when he arrived. On the veranda of the main office building, three young men in handcuffs sat huddled together.

"*Vapfana*," Tsvubvu said to the young constables outside. "Can one of you take me to your commanding officer?"

The officers looked at him and then one of them left the others and led him inside. The station's commanding officer was sitting behind his desk eating a doughnut when they entered his office. Without even waiting for his colleague to welcome him, Tsvubvu pulled a chair and made himself comfortable.

"Your face looks familiar," he said to his surprised host.

The man quickly recovered and smiled. "It should," he said. "We trained together. Don't you remember? My name is Muramba."

Tsvubvu remained silent for a moment. "Of course," he finally said. "I do remember now. You are the one who snored like a pig when we were at the academy."

In the next room someone giggled. Inspector Muramba puffed and shifted in his chair and then forced a smile.

"So, how can I be of help Chief Inspector Tsvubvu?" he said.

"Well," Tsvubvu paused and cleared his throat. "There is a case we are currently investigating involving a man who was shot in front of his house in Zengeza. HQ called and informed me that the slugs found in the deceased man matched those found in another victim who was shot at the Masawu flats five years ago. They said we should share intel and collaborate on this case."

Inspector Muramba scratched his forehead. "I understand," he said. "But this is going to take some time. Could you give us a day or two while we go through what we have on the Masawu flats case?"

An angry frown appeared on Chief Inspector Tsvubvu's face. He shook his head. "No, that won't do," he said. "I am not interested in hearing bureaucratic procedures Muramba. Just assign a detective to the case and I will do the same. Do you even have capable detectives here?"

Inspector Muramba shifted on his seat. He looked deeply offended. He opened his mouth to say something and then checked himself. "Wait here. I will be back in a minute," he said and left the office. He came back a couple of minutes later, being followed by a lanky young officer. "This is detective Mutipitipi," he declared. "He is the one you will be working with. I have already briefed him about the case." Detective Mutipitipi saluted, "It's an honour to meet you, sir," he said.

"Oh no, the honour is mine detective." Chief Inspector Tsvubvu said. "I want you to come to St Mary's Police station tomorrow morning. Our stations will be working together on this case. It has taken priority over all cases we currently have. We need to catch this killer before he strikes again. Your partner will be waiting for you. Do you understand?"

"Yes, sir."

"Okay. That's all Detective."

Mutipitipi saluted and left, leaving the two inspectors on their own.

"Do you think two officers will be enough to handle this case?" Inspector Muramba asked.

Chief Inspector Tsvubvu stood to leave. "I think they will. For now, let's assign two officers. We will monitor them and see how they fare," he said.

The moment he left Inspector Muramba's office, Mutipitipi went straight looking for the case file, which contained the details of the Masawu murder case. He liked investigating cases, for him investigating wasn't work. It was an exciting hobby. It did not take long for him to find the file. He carefully removed it from the shelf and then headed to his desk, where he took his time going through every detail regarding the case.

"So you've been assigned another one, huh?"

Mutipitipi raised his head to see who had talked. It was Tsunga, an officer from the CID Drugs Section. He was in the company of a young female officer. Everyone around the station knew Tsunga. He was one of the most handsome officers at the Mbare police station; this made him popular among the ladies.

"Yes indeed, I have been assigned a hot one," Mutipitipi said smiling. "It seems that the bosses are desperate to have this one solved as soon as possible."

"We will be rooting for you," Tsine, who specialised in serious fraud cases, interjected.

"Thanks. I just hope that we'll be able to solve this one soon."

"So, are you working alone on this one?" Tsunga asked.

"I will be working with someone from St Marys, but I haven't met the person yet."

"Well, I wish you all the luck," Tsunga remarked, heading for the exit. He was following the lady officer he had been talking with. Mutipitipi looked on indifferently as the man walked out. Unlike his colleague, he wasn't much of a ladies' man. Being a champion in matters of love had never been on the list of his top priorities. Alone again, with no one disturbing him, he looked back on his file and continued reading. It contained some details which he found interesting. The officers who worked on the case had come up with robbery as the motive. It made sense then since the first victim had been robbed of all his money. But now that the gun had been used again in Zengeza, Mutipitipi was beginning to have some doubts. Why had these two men been specifically targeted? He wondered. What was so special about them, which could have made someone want to kill them? These men were not rich, and from the few details he learned, nothing had been taken from the last victim.

File in hand, he left his desk and rushed back to Inspector Muramba's office. He wanted to talk to Chief Inspector Tsvubvu; there were many things he wanted to ask the Chief Inspector, things that needed clarity. When he reached the office, he was disappointed to find that the two Inspectors had already left. What was he going to do now? He pondered desperately. He could not wait for tomorrow. He needed some answers, and he needed them now. Walking back to his desk, he started planning his next move. He wasn't going to get the answers he needed if he remained in the office. It was better to start the investigations on his own for now. He would update his partner tomorrow if he found out anything useful. He headed straight home, where he removed his uniform and changed into civilian clothes. His experiences so far had taught him that most people were intimidated by the police but were likely to warm up to a private investigator. Having packed everything he needed for his investigation, he went straight to the Masawu flats. The sun was about to go down when he reached the place. A lot of youngsters were outside playing. Mutipitipi looked at them in awe. He knew he was looking at the purest of souls. Despite everything going on, including the economic hardships, they seemed to be in high spirits.

Playing in his head how he would conduct himself, he entered the housing block where the murder took place. He had high hopes of finding information, but the optimism slowly faded away when he started asking the people who lived in the housing block questions regarding the murder. Most of the people he talked to did not know anything about the incident. Who could blame them though? It had been five years since the murder had happened. To add to the complication, some people were new to the complex. But even then, there had to be some families who knew something, Mutipitipi reasoned. He continued to ask, but no one seemed to know anything. He had lost hope and was exiting the housing block when he bumped into a man staggering to enter. You didn't have to be a rocket scientist to tell that the fella was coming from the bar. He reeked of booze. Mutipitipi sincerely stopped the man and introduced himself as a private investigator. He told the man that he was investigating the murder of one John who had been shot in that complex five years ago.

"I knew John!" the man exclaimed.

"I am happy to hear that. So were you two friends?" Mutipitipi asked, feeling relieved that he had finally found someone who knew the victim.

"No," the drunkard shook his head. "We were not friends, but we used to bump into each other now and then. Hey, do you have any cigarettes on you? "

"No, I don't smoke. Were you here when the shooting occurred?"

The man shook his head again, "I was not here at the time. You see, a brother of mine had died. So when the shooting happened, I had travelled back to my roots for his funeral," Mutipitipi nodded.

"So is there anyone who still lives in this building or nearby who was there when the man was murdered?"

The drunkard thought for a moment, then shook his head. Mutipitipi remained quiet for a moment, thinking. This conversation wasn't yielding any useful information. He was coming out empty-handed here. He desperately needed something, anything that could somehow help him. "Is there anyone you know who might have had beef with him at the time?" he finally asked.

The drunkard shook his head, "not that I know of. If he had, well, he kept it to himself. John was one of those people we could call a closed book."

"I hear that he ran a successful shop. Wasn't there anyone who might have been jealous of him because of his success?"

The drunkard laughed. "A successful shop? There was no successful shop. The shop was just a cover up."

"Cover up for what?"

"Well, John was more of a hustler. Not many people know this, though, except his customers, but the man sold some exquisite weed."

"Weed?" Mutipitipi asked with immense interest.

"Yes. He sold some good stuff indeed, the sweetest weed I have ever come across," the drunkard said. Mutipitipi smiled. This was the information he had been searching for all along. That afternoon when he read John's file, nothing had been mentioned about drugs. His gut feeling told him he was now on to something. After asking a few more questions, he thanked the man and headed home. He was in high spirits. The pieces were now coming together nicely. That night, he cooked his dinner thinking about the case while whistling

George Michael's careless whisper. It appealed to the romantic in him.

The next morning, he woke up and headed straight to his office. He wanted to recover the file on John's murder, which he wanted to show the other officer he would partner with on the case. When he entered the building, Tsunga, Tsine and another female officer, Detective Ruzivo, were already inside, making some tea.

"Did you find anything interesting?" Tsine asked.

"Well, I uncovered something fascinating alright," Mutipitipi said thoughtfully. "I leant that John was a drug dealer."

"Are you certain? Who told you that?" Tsunga queried.

"Well, I met this drunkard at the flats last night. He used to be John's customer, he is the one who told me. You know as well as I do that people who are intoxicated seldom lie."

"That's right," Detective Ruzivo said, laughing. She approached Mutipitipi and handed him a cup of tea. "So you are now heading to Chitungwiza, I presume?"

"Yes," Mutipitipi said as he received the cup. He took a sip and frowned, "your tea is horrible," he remarked and put the cup on the table.

Tsunga and Tsine laughed loudly, while Ruzivo froze for a moment, an angry frown on her face. "You always have been an ungrateful bastard, you know that?" she finally barked. "And you're a terrible cook," Mutipitipi shot back and walked out of the building.

He immediately walked towards Simon Mazorodze road, searching for transport. It did not take him long to find a car that was heading to town. The lady driver was eating some buns. She offered him some, and he gladly accepted. The buns were so delicious that he asked for the recipe. The lady laughed and told him that she had bought them. She later dropped him in the CBD, where he boarded a kombi to Chitungwiza. The hour hand was racing towards 9 am when he reached St Mary's Police Station. As he reached the station, he began to feel dizzy and weak.

"Detective Mutipitipi, you are late. I expected to see you here at exactly eight," the Chief inspector thundered when the young detective entered his office.

"I am sorry sir," Mutipitipi said apologetically. "It won't happen again," he said.

"Wait for me here while I go and get your partner," Tsvubvu instructed as he walked out of the room. Mutipitipi nodded. He was now sweating and feeling dizzier. What was wrong with him? He pondered.

"Detective Mutipitipi. This is Detective Dohwe. She is one of our finest officers. She will be your partner on this case," Chief Inspector Tsvubvu said when he returned in to the office.

Mutipitipi turned his head and faced the other officer. She was a young woman with bright eyes. "My partner is a woman?" Mutipitipi mumbled. "Is that a problem? Don't tell me you are a sexist?" Chief Inspector Tsvubvu said.

Mutipitipi did not reply.

"Is he okay? He looks sick to me," Detective Dohwe remarked as she closely inspected Mutipitipi's face. At that moment, Mutipitipi fell off his chair and landed heavily on the floor.

"Someone call an ambulance!" Chief inspector Tsvubvu shouted.

Chapter 18

Nurse Kunatsa was right. Talking to other people helps. It especially helps when you talk to positive people, people who are in your situation, and people who are trying to make something out of their lives. I guess that is why some people go to therapy. Talking to people who truly care is like being relieved of a heavy load after a very long and arduous journey. I discovered this when I started attending the support group meetings. Being involved with the group made me hopeful again. It healed me inside and made me view the future with a positive mind. I found myself drinking less, and I also stopped using drugs altogether. The only thing I found hard to stop was selling them. I couldn't stop. I just couldn't. The drug deals gave me a lot of money. With the money I was making, I was now able to buy myself furniture, some clothes, and decent food. My room, which had been empty, was starting to feel homely again. The damning fact I could not run away from during that time was that the drug money sustained me. Stopping the trade meant a trip to poverty and misery.

Things were changing, and they were changing fast. The worst part was that things were not changing for the better. Life was becoming harder and harder. Living in the city was becoming more and more expensive. The price of things like bread and cooking oil was going up, and there was no sign of stabilisation. Because of these economic woes, some days I would miss home so badly that I would contemplate going back. Life in the city is hard. It is simple only to those with deep pockets.

In the city, almost everything is bought— water, lights, and food.

By contrast, in the rural areas where I come from, you don't have to crack your head thinking about bills. If you are tired of eating vegetables, you can go fishing or mice-trapping. It takes one who has lived in both environments to really appreciate rural life.

I was lying in my bed one morning, thinking about what I was going to do with myself for the rest of that day, when Victor suddenly budged into my room. He stood in the middle of the room. He looked excited.

"It's finally happening today," he said.

"What's happening today?" I asked, confused.

"The elopement. Me and my girl, we are going to do it today."

I remained quiet for a moment. Having done something similar to this before, I wasn't sure what to say. "I guess congratulations are in order," I finally said.

"Damn right they are. You have no idea how happy I am. I spent a lot of time chasing after that girl," he said as he sat down. "I didn't come here to brag though, I came because I need your help."

"My help?"

"Yes. We are doing it tonight, I want you to accompany me to her house to fetch her."

I thought for a moment. Going to take someone's daughter in the middle of the night isn't a walk in the park. It's serious business. I had heard of some guys losing their precious teeth because of this. Also, Victor had previously shown me his father-in-law. The man had made an impression on me. He seemed to be someone who was not to be messed with.

"I don't know, man," I finally said, shaking my head, "that father-in-law of yours seems to be crazy."

"Really? That's all you are going to say? You owe me one, you know that right?"

I nodded. I knew I owed him a lot. Most of the time, when I encountered a problem, he was the person I ran to. "What time do you want to go?" I finally asked.

"Now that's more like it," Victor said, smiling, "I will come to get you at around midnight."

I spent the rest of that day at the market selling fruits and vegetables and some weed now and then. Like always, I made more money on this side business than from selling my vegetables and fruits. Later, as I headed home, I passed through a bar and indulged in a few drinks. I was very nervous; drinking was my desperate attempt at calming my nerves.

As promised, Victor arrived at my house at around midnight. We immediately headed to Mbare National, a housing area located southwest of Mbare Musika. It took us about half an hour or so to reach the house. When we arrived, everything was dead quiet. I felt a bit relieved when I saw that no one was loitering in the streets. Everything seemed to be going to plan. Like they had agreed, the girl had left the gate unlocked. Victor opened it, making sure not to make any sound and then signalled me to follow, but I shook my head, whispering in his ear that I was going to remain outside as a lookout. It was a bit wintry outside, and I was already regretting my arrogance of coming without a jacket. Alone outside, I stood, shivering, glancing in every direction now and then to see if anyone was coming. Having been standing outside for a minute or so, I finally heard some footsteps running towards me.

"Stop! Stop right there!" A male voice suddenly barked. I realised we had been discovered. At that moment, Victor and his girl suddenly emerged from the concrete wall surrounding the house. He immediately handed me one of the bags he was carrying, and we began to flee. As we left, we heard some commotion and shouting behind us. We increased our pace and ran as fast as we could, only slowing down when we realised no one was pursuing us.

"What happened back there?" I asked Victor when we were about to reach his house. "My father-in-law happened," he declared. "The old man saw us as we were about to leave the house."

"Well, I owed you one, but now I think that I have paid my debt in full," I said, handing him back the bag he had given me earlier.

"Thanks a lot, words cannot even begin to describe how grateful I am right now," he said, shaking my hand.

"Don't mention it," I told him. "I think it's time I head back home."

"What?! Now? I can't let you do that. What if muggers attack you along the way? Stay. Rest here while the sun comes out. I would not forgive myself if anything bad were to happen to you, please, stay," he insisted.

I nodded and finally agreed to stay; it made sense. Mbare is notorious for muggings. Loitering alone at night is definitely a bad idea. Victor and I knew this well. Almost every day when we were at the marketplace, we heard of some unlucky person who would have lost their wallet to pickpockets or someone who would have been robbed. We also bumped into the offenders now and then. Being involved in the drug business, it was impossible not to meet these people. As they say, it takes a criminal to know another. The truth is, the criminal world is like an ecosystem—a system where different criminals unite and depend on each other to survive. The muggers and pickpockets came to us when they needed weed. As a result, our business thrived, and since they usually got hooked on the drug, a continuous relationship usually resulted. On the other hand, we, the drug peddlers, would go to the muggers and pickpockets if we wanted cheap gadgets and other goods which we knew they could get. Nothing is for free, so we would also have to pay them for these goods. It's a vicious cycle, one which has been going on for ages.

When we arrived at Victor's home his mother received us warmly and made us tea. She had mixed emotions about the whole thing, but all in all, she seemed happy about the new development.

We stayed up and conversed until 6 am. By then, I was feeling very tired. I finally said my goodbyes and headed home. Having walked for a couple of hundreds of metres, I noticed a group of apoplectic men coming towards me. A man was leading them, who I quickly realised was Victor's father-in-law. His face looked livid, and from the way he was talking to the mob, I could tell that Victor would be in very hot soup if no one warned him. How did he know where Victor lived? I wondered.

Once we passed each other, I took another path that led to Victor's home and ran back as fast as I could. I arrived just before the mob and met Victor as he was leaving the house with a plastic bag in his hand. I quickly grabbed his hand and dragged him to the back of his house.

"What are you doing?" he asked, surprised.

"They're here," I said as I continued to drag him to the back.

"Who is here?" he asked, confused.

"Your in-laws! They are here. From the way they were talking, it doesn't look like they are here for a rave. You better hide," I advised.

"But where?" he asked, looking around. The mob was now arriving. Without thinking, we both scrambled into a nearby mango tree.

"Where is that bastard?!" Victor's father-in-law thundered as the mob approached the house.

"Where is he?"

There was a lot of commotion in the front of the yard. The mob wanted Victor, and they wanted him badly. They entered the house and started searching for him in every room.

Victor's mother, realising she could not reason with them, started crying.

"Kundai! Pack all your things now!" Victor's father-in-law shouted. "I will never, I repeat, I will never allow you to marry that bastard, you hear me, never!"

"I am not going anywhere with you?" Kundai responded angrily to her father.

"What?! What did you say to me?"

"I said I am not going anywhere with you, father," Kundai replied stubbornly.

The father laughed loudly. "You are going home," he declared. "You are going. I don't care if I will have to drag you all the way back. You are going back home with me. You hear?"

"I am not going," Kundai stood her ground.

I heard what sounded like a slap, and a few moments later, Kundai started crying. She continued resisting, though, I heard the men who had come with her father struggling with her.

"This cannot continue," Victor suddenly declared, almost at the point of crying. "I need to go in there and fight for my girl," he said as he climbed down the tree.

"Don't," I said, clenching his hand. "If you go near those guys, they will disfigure you." I pleaded with him.

He pulled his hand away and climbed down the tree. I remained in the tree for a couple of seconds and then followed him. Maybe he was right, I thought. I had always been fearful when faced with situations like these; maybe it was now time to stand up and fight like my friend from childhood, Peter, who stood up to a bully and won. But how naive I was to think like that. Those guys were not fooling around. The moment they laid their eyes on us, well, all hell broke loose. In the Shona language, there is a saying that loosely translates to: a coward has no scars. A coward lives to tell the story. I guess I finally realised the meaning of this proverb when I came face to face with those men that day. They were angry, and to say we were given a beating would be an understatement. The guys wanted to kill us.

"Please don't harm my kids, please don't harm them." Victor's mom moaned and pleaded with the men while kneeling on the ground. They paid no attention to her and continued to punish us while we lay on the ground. I finally realised that I was going to get seriously injured if I didn't escape. The moment the opportunity arrived, I decided to make a run for it. Two of the men pursued me, but to no avail, I ran at the fastest pace I had ever run in my life. After about half a kilometre, my pursuers finally realised that they were never going to catch me; they gave up.

When I arrived home, I felt a bit depressed, and my whole body was numb. Although I was covered in dust, it never crossed my mind to have a bath. I was so exhausted that all I could think of was getting some sleep. The moment I threw myself on the bed, I quickly drifted to sleep. I slept almost for the whole of that day. When I finally woke up, the hour hand was way past five, heading towards six. With a strong will, I dragged myself out of bed and boiled some water for bathing on my one plate Kango stove. The bath made me feel a lot better, in fact, so better that I even thought of going to the market to sell my wares but later decided against it. I ended up staying in my room, listening to a short wave channel on my radio. They were discussing the English Premier League. For a few minutes, I listened attentively as the football pundits argued passionately about who they thought would win the league that season. Later, I changed to a music channel that was playing lively tunes. Laying on my bed, listening, I eventually departed to the world of dreams again. The next morning, I woke up feeling much better. Since I had not gone out the day before, many of my customers came looking for me. One of them, miserable Gudo, came in looking more sullen than usual. He was always miserable alright; desperate for some weed. The sad thing, though, was that he hardly had enough money to buy the drugs he needed, which made him even more miserable.

"What's bothering you, Gudo, my friend?" I asked him.

"Man, I am so sad right now. You haven't heard, have you?"

"What are you talking about?" I asked.

"Man, things that have happened are making me so low right now. It's about your friend Victor."

"What about him?"

"He is dead."

"What!" I jumped. "You are lying."

"No, I am not," Miserable Gudo declared. "He was found hanging from a mango tree behind his house by his mother early this morning. Man, I am feeling so miserable right now. I really need some weed. Do you have some?"

Chapter 19

Kam was busy enjoying the afternoon with his mother when he noticed a white Mazda B2200 pulling into his driveway. He had decided to spend the whole day with his mother. Mavis, the senior shop employee would be taking care of business today as she had always done before when he was not around at the shop. They were seated in the shade of the Jacaranda tree in their front yard. With the cool shade, fine-looking flowers, Kam found the ambience very surreal. Everything felt good and looked perfect; that's until Maromo appeared.

He wasn't amused when he saw the man approaching his house. Why had Maromo come? He pondered. Although he had once visited Maromo's house, they had agreed that Maromo was not to set foot in his yard since this would result in his mother getting suspicious. He on the other hand, was allowed to visit Maromo because, well, Maromo's wife already knew about her husband's shenanigans.

"Mother, this man is my friend, his name is Maromo," Kam said when his business associate had offered his greetings.

"He is your friend? You have never mentioned his name before," Eva asked curiously.

"It just never came up, I guess," Kam replied, avoiding his mother's gaze.

Eva looked at Maromo with intense interest. Who was this strange man who her son was claiming to be a friend? She wondered.

"Please, sit down and have tea with us, Mr Maromo," she finally said.

Maromo shook his head, "Thanks, Mrs Kam but I am okay."

"Are you sure? I have been told I make great tea."

"I am okay, maam, really."

Eva smiled and nodded her head. "So, what is it that you do?" She finally asked.

"I am a businessman. I own a retail store."

"That's nice. So are you making money?"

"Not much, but I can't complain," Maromo responded.

"So, where do you operate from? Harare?"

"I operate from Chitungwiza," Maromo replied. He was now getting a little irritated. Kam's mother was asking too many questions. Anxious to get on with what he had come to see Kam for, he decided to end the conversation before it went any further. "I am sorry to have disturbed your beautiful afternoon Mrs Kam, but may I please steal your son for a moment?" he said.

"I don't see why not. Just make sure that he comes back home, will you," Eva said, smiling.

"You don't have to worry yourself about that," Maromo said, laughing.

Kam excused himself from his mother and followed Maromo.

"You shouldn't have come here," he said as they walked to Maromo's car.

"I know," Maromo retorted. "I only came because something has happened. Get into the car. We need to find a safe spot where we can talk."

Kam climbed into the B2200 and they drove off. A few minutes later, Maromo finally stopped and parked his car on the side of the road.

"So what's so important that it couldn't wait?" Kam asked.

"Well, one of my boys died last night, he hanged himself?"

"Why?"

"What do you think? It's because of a girl of course. He and his girl had eloped the night before last but yesterday morning the girl's father came to his house with a mob and assaulted him. They also took away the girl," Maromo said.

"Is there a reason why you are telling me this?" Kam asked.

"A police officer came to my house this morning."

"A police officer?!" Kam exclaimed.

"Relax. It's not like that. The officer is Delight's man on the inside."

"Well, that's comforting. What did he want?" Kam said, sounding very relieved.

"He wanted to warn me about the kid," Maromo replied. "He told me that the police are likely to snoop around because they found a lot of weed in his room."

Kam shrugged. He didn't see why Maromo seemed so worked up. "So why should we care? We didn't kill him."

"That's true, but the problem is that there is this friend of his who knows my face and who I am. If the police somehow question him about the origins of the weed, he may likely crack. He is relatively new to the business. Do you see where I am going with this?"

Kam nodded, "you are afraid that he may end up selling us out."

"The possibility is very high."

Kam remained silent for a while. He did not like how things were currently going. It seemed as if they were now always fire-fighting. This was why he sometimes contemplated tapping out. He always found these moments to be draining. He could not believe this was happening.

They were currently on edge because of the Zengeza incident. Another one at this point was not something he wanted to hear at all. "So, what are you suggesting we should do?" he finally asked.

"I think we should get rid of him before he talks."

"Get rid of him?! Are you serious? Don't you see that this would create an even bigger problem?" Kam protested.

"You need to understand something, my friend. If that boy talks, we are done. You hear me? Done! And if that boy talks, trust me, I am not going to go down alone. I will definitely take you with me. I hope you understand that."

"Can't we just talk to him? There is a chance he might be loyal."

Maromo shook his head. "The kid has to go my friend. He has to go."

Kam covered his face with his hands. This couldn't be happening. How many people would have to die to protect this secret of theirs? He pondered. He was starting to get tired of it all.

"So, what exactly are you planning to do?" he finally asked.

"We will just have to knock him out and bury him where no one will ever find him," Maromo declared.

"The police officer, is he on board?"

Maromo nodded, "of course he is. He even offered to help."

Kam just nodded and remained quiet. Although he did not agree with Maromo's ways of solving problems, he realised that he was way more terrified of going to jail to care. He was currently being faced with two options: choosing himself, or the young man. Kam decided that he was going to choose himself. After all, whoever said that the world was fair? The world is a place where the strong will always prey on the weak. Besides, even if he was to protest, nothing was likely to change the boy's fate. There were many people vested in the business, people who would do anything to keep the boy silent. The boy's fate had already been sealed the moment he decided to join the drug business. Kam got back into Maromo's car, and the two men immediately headed for Chitungwiza. When they arrived, they tracked Yots in the two shopping centres he liked to hang around— Chigovanyika and Huruyadzo, but they could not find him. However, as if by luck, as they were driving along Chaminuka road on their way back to the city, Maromo suddenly noticed one of Yots' drinking buddies walking along the road.

"Hey! Have you seen Yots today?" he called out to the man.

"He is at Makoni," the man shouted back. "I saw him boarding a kombi which was heading there this morning."

This was good news. After hearing this, Maromo immediately stepped on the accelerator and headed for the small shopping centre. It took him only about 20 minutes to reach there. Having driven around the shopping centre for a while, the two men finally found Yots in one of the small bars at the edge of the shopping centre. He was busy enjoying his favourite beer while playing darts. The young man was currently leading in the game he was playing. Maromo and Kam decided to wait for him until the match was over. A lot of money was on the line. Many people had bet their money on the match so dragging Yots out before the game was finished was likely to cause a huge and unnecessary brawl. The two men made themselves comfortable on one of the benches and looked on as Yots destroyed his opponent. The young man was quite good. He was playing exceptionally well. Within a couple of minutes, he had defeated his opponent.

"What did you think of my performance?" the young man asked as he approached Maromo and Kam after the game had ended.

"You did very well. I did not know you were that good at playing Darts." Kam remarked. "I am. It's good to see you here," Yots said, grinning. He paused for a moment looking at the two men. "I don't think you came all the way here just to see me play darts, did you? What really brought you here?" he finally asked.

"We have a problem."

"What kind of problem?" Yots asked.

"There is someone who needs to be gotten rid of immediately," Maromo said with a low voice.

"You can't be serious," Yots moaned. "You want to do that again? Is the person even that dangerous?"

Maromo nodded his head. "I suspect he is about to sell us out."

Yots silently rubbed his head for a moment, thinking. "Well, if that's the case, then I guess it can't be helped, can it? So where does this unfortunate fella live?"

"We cannot discuss that here," Maromo responded. "Why don't we go back to the car where we can discuss this without looking over our shoulders?"

Yots agreed, and the three men exited the bar and got into the B2200, where Maromo laid out his plan. After almost half an hour of conversing, the three men finally reached a consensus on how they would carry out their plan. They drove to a nearby hardware and bought two picks and two shovels.

"Why did we buy the extra tools? We are only three," Yots asked, looking confused.

"It's because someone will be accompanying us," Maromo retorted.

"Who?"

"Be patient. You are going to meet him soon."

After the tools were safely in the back, Maromo sped the Mazda truck towards Mbare. They reached their target's house at around half past five. When they drove slowly past the place, they noticed that no one seemed to be at the house. Though they wanted to approach it, the three men realised it would be foolish to approach the target's house themselves. Rather, it would make sense to send someone who looked harmless. A group of young boys played a plastic ball a couple of metres away from them. Maromo waved his hand and called one of the boys to the car.

"Hey boy, do you want to make some quick money?" he asked. The young boy vigorously nodded his head.

"Good. I want you to go to that house and ask for the young man who lives there," Maromo said, pointing at the house. "If he is there, tell him that we are his customers and we are waiting for him," he added, handing the boy some money. The young boy ran to the house and knocked at the door, and a middle-aged woman answered the knock. After a few moments of conversing with the lady, the boy came back running.

"The woman who lives there said the man you are looking for is at a funeral," the boy said breathlessly.

"A funeral?"

"Yes."

Maromo nodded his head. Of course, he had to be at his friend's funeral. Why hadn't he thought of that earlier? He wondered. He reached into his pockets and pulled out more money. "Would you mind coming in the car with us? We are not going that far. I want you to do one more thing for me," he said, handing the boy more money. For a moment, the boy looked into the car suspiciously.

"It is okay. We are not going that far," Maromo said reassuringly. The boy nodded and finally agreed to enter the car. Yots, who had been sitting in the front, got out to make way for the boy. He opened the truck's canopy and sat in the back. Maromo drove to the house where the funeral was taking place. A lot of people were sitting outside when they reached the house. As they drove past it, Maromo slowed down. "My boy, do you see that young man wearing a red shirt?" he asked, pointing. The young boy nodded his head. "Good, I want you to go and tell him that we are customers and we urgently want to talk to him. Make sure that no one hears you. Whisper in his ear if you can." The boy nodded and exited the car. As he started running towards the crowd, Maromo looked on and smiled.

"I told you," he said, turning to Kam. "I knew this would work."

Chapter 20

Mutipitipi woke up feeling a bit light-headed and confused. Looking around him, he quickly noticed there were white sheets everywhere. What was happening? Where was he? He pondered. As he was busy struggling with these thoughts, a lady dressed in white suddenly came into the room.

"Where am I?" he asked.

The lady gave him a warm smile. "Don't you worry, sir, you are okay. You are in very capable hands."

Mutipitipi raised his head and looked around. A lot of strange bottles and containers were on the table beside him. What was this place? What had happened to him? He wondered.

"Where am I?" he asked the lady again.

"You are at Chitungwiza Central Hospital," the lady replied.

Mutipitipi remained quiet for a moment, thinking. Vivid images began to flood his mind. He remembered now. He had been at St Mary's police station, waiting for his partner. What had happened then? He could not remember. There seemed to be a blank slate that he failed to recall. So he was now in hospital? How had this happened?

"How did I end up here? Who came with me?"

"Your colleagues came with you yesterday. You were very sick and unconscious when you came in."

"What?! Yesterday? You mean I came here yesterday?"

"Yes," the nurse answered calmly.

How could this have happened? What disease might he have contracted? Mutipitipi pondered. At that moment, as he was mulling over his present situation, another lady suddenly came into the room.

She was wearing plain clothes and looked a lot more opulent than the nurse.

She introduced herself as his doctor.

"How are you feeling, Mr Mutipitipi?" she asked warmly.

"I am feeling fine now. What happened to me?" Mutipitipi asked.

"You were poisoned."

"Poisoned?!"

"Yes. Tests show that you ingested cyanide. We found traces of it in your system. Fortunately, the amount you took was not large enough to cause a fatality. You are a very lucky man Mr Mutipitipi. Would you have any idea how the poison entered into your system?" Mutipitipi shook his head.

"I don't know, doctor. I really don't know," he said. So he had been poisoned? How? When? "If you had to make a guess, when do you think I was poisoned?" he asked.

"I would definitely say around yesterday morning," the doctor said confidently.

Mutipitipi remained quiet, thinking. If what the lady doctor had told him was true, then it meant that there were two people that he would need to talk to. These included Detective Ruzivo and the lady who had offered him a lift. These two women were the only people who had given him something to eat yesterday. Why would any one of them want to kill him? He pondered. He needed to talk to these women urgently. He wasn't likely going to have any problems talking to Ruzivo, but the other woman was going to be difficult to find. It seemed that someone did not want him to investigate the case.

"Mr Mutipitipi, are you quite certain you are feeling okay?" the doctor asked warmly.

Mutipitipi nodded his head. "I am okay, doctor. I am just trying to figure out who poisoned me. So, when should I expect to be discharged?"

The doctor looked at the papers she was holding. "The nurses will monitor you for the rest of the day. I think we may be able to let you go as early as tomorrow."

Mutipitipi nodded his head and remained quiet. Tomorrow?! But he could not wait for tomorrow! He needed to leave, now. However, arguing with the doctor for an early discharge was unlikely going to bear any fruit. If he was to leave today, he realised that he needed a plan of escape. The instant, the two women exited the room. He quietly got off the bed. How was he going to exit the building unnoticed? He wondered. The window? He went to the window and slid open the curtains. If he was to leave now, it definitely wasn't going to be through that way. The window was barricaded with some very solid burglar bars. What was he going to do now? He opened the door, peeped outside and found himself looking into the corridor. There were a lot of people going in and out of the building. Could he sneak out undetected?

Mutipitipi thought he could. He walked back to the bed, where he picked his wallet and wristwatch, which had been placed on the table. His wristwatch showed that the time was 12:30 pm. Not one to waste time, he quickly wore his uniform, exited the room and walked calmly towards the exit. No one gave him much thought. The nurses he passed in the corridor were too busy with their patients to notice. Within a few seconds, he was out of the building. The sun was high up in the sky. Its rays hit his skin and made him feel alive again. Mutipitipi began jogging towards the exit gate. He knew it wasn't going to be long before the nurses responsible for him discovered that he was missing in his room. When he reached the tarred road adjacent to the hospital, he frantically waved at a kombi headed towards the city of Harare, and it stopped. The kombi dropped him near the St Marys Police Station, at the T junction of Seke and Chaminuka Road. From there, he walked into the police station. He found Dohwe standing at the entrance gate, talking to another police officer.

"What are you doing here?" she said when she saw him. "Do you realise that people back at the hospital are worried sick about you? They called a few minutes ago informing us that you had disappeared. Do you realise how much trouble you are in right now?"

Mutipitipi shrugged. "I know, but I am not really concerned about that right now. Did you find anything new on our case?"

"What case? You mean the one we were supposed to investigate? Don't bother yourself; it has been reassigned to other people."

"What?! They can't do that!" he exclaimed.

"I am afraid to say this my friend, but they can. You and I know that."

"Well, if that's the case, I will continue investigating on my own. It seems the killer does not want me to continue investigating this case. This means I am on to something."

"What makes you say that?"

"I was poisoned. That's what made me sick yesterday."

"For real!" Dohwe exclaimed, seemingly shocked.

"That's what the doctor told me. Can you give me the address of the victim's house? There is something I need to verify."

"Why don't you wait for the Chief Inspector? If you plead with him, he may reconsider his decision."

Mutipitipi shook his head. "You don't understand. I need to do this right now."

Dohwe sighed and reached into her pockets, where she pulled out a piece of paper and a pen. "You didn't get this from me," she said, writing the address on the paper and handing it to him. Glancing at the paper, he realised that the distance to the house was walkable. Mutipitipi knew Chitungwiza fairly well, it was his hometown, the place where he had lived for almost half of his life. He quickly bade farewell to Dohwe and started his journey. Having walked for about a kilometre or so, he suddenly realised how hungry he was. What would someone recovering from poisoning eat? He wondered and quickly remembered that someone had told him that bananas and rice worked wonders. As he continued walking, he noticed a small store beside the road selling some fruits and approached it.

"Hello my son. What do you want to buy this fine afternoon?" An edentulous elderly woman manning the shop greeted him with a broad warm smile.

"I want some bananas, please," he said.

"How many?"

"I think five will do."

The woman picked the bananas and packed them neatly in a plastic bag. She even added an extra one gratis. As he looked at her, her face warm and caring, he was immediately reminded of his own Grandmother. Mutipitipi paid for the bananas and resumed his journey. The bananas, which were very sweet and tender, made him feel better. After about half an hour, he reached the victim's house. On the veranda sat two dreadlocked young men. The two young men were smoking a joint. When they noticed him, they quickly chucked it away.

"Wagwan, my brothers? Weh yu deh pan?" Mutipitipi greeted them, smiling.

"Nagwan my man." One of the young men replied enthusiastically.

"I am afraid that's the only Patois I know," he said, laughing. "My name is Mutipitipi. I am the one who is investigating the unfortunate incident that happened here."

"What do you people want again?" One of the young men complained. "Your colleagues came here and harassed my wife's brother. I thought she told you everything you wanted to know?"

So the new guys on the case had already come here? Had they found anything useful yet? He wondered. Their coming here was now likely to make his job a lot more difficult. How was he going to make these young men open up to him now? He pondered. Realising that he would not get the information he wanted if the young men remained apprehensive, he walked to the spot they had thrown the joint and picked it up.

"Do you have matches?" he asked calmly.

"What?!" both young men asked, tense and poised for flight.

"Matches. I need matches. Do you have some?"

The two looked at each other before handing him a box of matches. Mutipitipi lit the joint and took a very big puff before exhaling. In that instant, the young men's fear turned into surprise, and the surprise turned into admiration.

"Man! You are so cool!" one of the young men exclaimed as he bumped his fist with the other.

"Am I?"

"Yes you are, my brother."

"So, what are your names, gentlemen?"

"I am Ino. This brother beside me here is Taz."

"Very well. So, Taz and Ino, are you related to the victim?"

"I am related to him," Ino responded.

"Good," Mutipitipi said, smiling broadly. The joint was something else. He started wondering if his attempt to impress the young men had been wise. He was already beginning to feel funny.

"So, Ino, this is the deal. I need you to tell me everything, and I mean everything. I want you to know that I am not here to arrest anyone. I am not here for that. I am here to help you and your family find some much-needed closure. Do you understand?"

Ino nodded, "I do."

"Excellent," Mutipitipi remarked. Things now seemed to be going smoothly. "So you and your brother, were you close?"

"Yes, we were very close," Ino said as he pulled another joint from his pocket. He lit it and took a deep puff before handing it to his friend Taz.

"Was your brother employed?" "No." Ino shook his head.

"How then did he make a living?" Mutipitipi asked.

"He was very good with his hands. He did some temporary jobs now and then. That's how he made his money."

"Is that all he did?"

"Yes," Ino nodded.

Mutipitipi remained quiet for a moment. Why would an honest and hardworking man end up with two bullet wounds? He wondered. That didn't make sense at all. Something was up. There was definitely something that Ino had left out.

"So, how was your brother's marriage?"

"What do you mean?" Ino queried.

"I am trying to find out if he was happy in his marriage."

"Of course. My brother was very happy."

"Are you sure? Wasn't he involved with anyone? Anyone who could have been someone's wife? Many men these days are involved in extramarital activities."

Ino laughed. "No," he said, shaking his head. "My brother wasn't like that. He was very happy in his marriage. If he had been involved with anyone, I would have known. He and his wife loved each other very much. It's a shame that she wasn't here when this evil person attacked him. Otherwise, this would have been a very different story."

If what this young man had told him was true, then this meant it couldn't have been a crime of passion, Mutipitipi decided. He just had to verify before reaching conclusions. Crimes of passion were on the rise these days. Many people were assaulting and even killing each other due to infidelity. As a police officer, he heard of these cases almost every day. There was, however, a question that he hadn't asked yet. A question that was nagging him. He stood up and made as if to leave.

"I noticed you have some very good weed?" he said.

Ino smiled. "It's good isn't it?"

"Best weed I have ever had. Did your brother sell this?" Mutipitipi asked.

Ino stopped smiling and looked down. He took a deep puff from the joint before he talked. "Things are hard for people like us these days. A man has to do whatever he can to survive."

"So you are saying he sold weed?"

"Yes, he did."

Mutipitipi scratched his chin. What were the chances that this could just be a coincidence? He wondered.

"Wasn't he having problems with someone because of this? A disagreement with his supplier or another seller maybe," he asked.

Ino shook his head. "No, not at all."

"Are you sure?"

"I am certain," Ino said with conviction. "My brother would never have hidden something like that from me, but….."

"But what?"

"Before he died, he mentioned that there was someone who had bought some weed from him who looked suspicious."

"What did the person look like?" Mutipitipi queried.

"He didn't say. He only mentioned that the guy was driving a white Mazda B2200 with a broken headlight."

Mutipitipi nodded his head and wrote this down. Who knows, he thought, small details like this could come in handy in the future. After he felt that he had all the information he needed, Mutipitipi bade farewell to the two young men and left straight for Mbare. He was now desperate to see Detective Ruzivo. He passed through his house, where he got into clean clothes and headed to his colleagues' place. When he reached Detective Ruzivo's house, the sun was about to set. Her younger sister was in the front yard, washing her school uniform.

"Is your sister around?" he asked as he approached her.

"No," the young girl shook her head. "She has gone to a funeral."

"Who died?"

"One of her church member's sons. He hanged himself yesterday."

"That's saddening," Mutipitipi said thoughtfully. "Can you take me to the house? I need to talk to your sister."

The young girl nodded, locked the front door and led Mutipitipi to the house where the funeral was underway. When they reached the house, he noticed that a lot of people were sitting outside in the front yard. Mutipitipi decided to remain behind in the street while the girl entered to call her sister. After a couple of minutes, the young girl came back, with Ruzivo following closely behind her.

"What is so important that you had to drag my young sister here?" Ruzivo asked with an angry tone.

Mutipitipi did not immediately respond. He remained silent, closely observing how Ruzivo was behaving. He noticed she did not seem terrified to see him. She didn't even seem surprised to see him either. She didn't seem like someone guilty of anything at all. Either she was very good at acting, or she was just innocent.

"I need to ask you something, that cup of tea you gave me yesterday morning. Are you the one who made it?"

"No, I just took it. Someone had already made the cup. Maybe it was Tsine or Tsunga, I don't know. It was just a prank. I was just being naughty. I wanted to annoy the person who had prepared the cup."

"So you mean you just took the cup, and you don't even know the person who made it?" Mutipitipi asked, looking at Ruzivo. He wasn't buying her explanation at all.

"Yes," she responded innocently. Mutipitipi didn't say anything. He remained quiet and stared at her. "Don't you look at me like that!" Ruzivo exclaimed. "You know very well that everyone at the office sometimes poaches tea now and then. Well, almost everyone maybe except you. Why are you fussing about it anyway?"

"I am fussing about it because someone poisoned me yesterday?"

"What?!"

"You heard me. Someone tried to kill me yesterday. I spend the whole day and night in the hospital. The doctor told me that they found cyanide in my system."

"I am so sorry. I didn't know. No one had told me. You don't think that I am the one who poisoned you, do you?"

Mutipitipi shrugged, "who knows? No one can be trusted these days."

"Look, I was just trying to be nice to you. That's why I stole that cup of tea. I did it for you. I would never try to harm you. You know that, right?"

Mutipitipi thought for a bit. He and Ruzivo had always had a strange friendship. If he wasn't so much of a coward, the friendship could have developed into something much more a long time ago. She was one of the few people who had always stood by him at work when he had messed up. Besides, she had made tea for him many times before. If she had not poisoned him then, why would she do it now? He wondered. But then again, people can't be blindly trusted, no matter who they are. Some of the most respectable people end up doing the most unexpected of things. The fact that Ruzivo had pleaded her innocence wasn't enough to remove her from his list of suspects. Something was now bothering him, though. If Ruzivo had been truthful in what she had said, then this means there were two other suspects whom he needed to investigate. Investigating these two was going to be difficult. How would they react to the accusation? He wondered. And if they eventually turned out to be innocent, would they ever forgive him?

"So you do understand why I can't be the one who poisoned you, right?" Ruzivo was now saying.

"What?"

"Have you been listening to what I was saying?"

"Oh, yes. I was listening." Mutipitipi responded. He was, of course, lying through his teeth. All this time, she had been busy trying to argue her innocence, he had pretended to be listening. It was now becoming darker outside, he felt very tired. He had a long day tomorrow and was likely going to face some disciplinary action because of his conduct at the hospital. Considering where the time was, he felt there was nothing more he could do. It was now time to go home. As he was about to leave, something happened which immediately caught his attention. A white Mazda B2200 with a broken headlight slowly passed and parked a couple of metres ahead. When he saw it, many thoughts started running through his head. A white Mazda B2200 with a broken headlight! What were the odds? He wondered. He turned to Ruzivo. "The boy who died. What did he do for a living?" he asked.

"He was a vendor. Why do you ask?" Ruzivo said.

Mutipitipi remained silent and focused his attention on the Mazda B200. A young boy suddenly disembarked from the car and ran towards a group of young men sitting in the yard where the funeral was taking place. The boy approached a young man and whispered in his ear. Immediately after, the young man stood up and walked towards the white Mazda truck. When he reached it he talked to the driver for a minute or so, then moved to the back of the car, opened the canopy and climbed in. The Mazda immediately drove off. Seeing this, Mutipitipi immediately ran to a commuter omnibus that was parked beside the road near him. The driver of the kombi was busy talking to a young lady who was standing beside the vehicle. Mutipitipi immediately opened the door and jumped in.

"Hey, I am a police officer. Do you see that car?" he barked, pointing at the Mazda, which was about to disappear around the corner. The kombi driver could only manage to nod. "Good, follow it. Follow it now!"

Chapter 21

The news of Victor's death left me in a state of utter shock. I hadn't took him for someone who could kill himself. Maybe I should have done something more to help him yesterday, I thought. I was now filled with regret. I cried. It was all too late now. I went into my room and locked myself in. I was overwrought. I wanted to calm myself down.

After almost an hour, I finally unlocked my door and headed for Victor's home. When I arrived, I found out that his body had already been rushed to a mortuary to lay until the burial arrangements had been finalised. A lot of people were already at the house, offering their condolences to Victor's mother. I cried when I saw her. She was so sullen, and she looked completely devastated.

I spent that whole day at Victor's home. At around six, when the sun had just gone down, a young boy suddenly appeared beside me and whispered that there were a couple of customers who wanted to see me. "Customers?"

The boy nodded. "Follow me. I can take you to them," he said.

I stood up from where I was sitting and followed the boy. He led me to a car that was parked beside the road. These weren't customers. I recognised the car the moment I saw it. It was Maromo's car. What did he want? What was he thinking coming here in light of what had just happened? I pondered. Maromo wasn't alone. A man was sitting beside him who I had never seen before.

"Hi boss. What are you doing here?" I asked as I approached the car.

"I had to see you. What happened to your friend is a tragedy indeed. Are you okay?"

"No, I am not okay," I said.

"I understand. No one can be okay after something like this," he said. I could not help but notice that he was a little more polite to me today. What could be the purpose of his visit? I wondered. I looked at his companion and he quickly looked away. "Tichakunda, I need your help." Maromo finally said.

"My help?"

"Yes, I need you to help me bury something."

"But I am at a funeral. I can't just leave," I protested.

"Did you tell anyone that you were leaving?" Maromo queried.

"No," I said.

"Then that's fantastic," Maromo remarked happily. "You don't need to worry. I will bring you back in no time at all. No one will even notice you were gone."

What did Maromo want to bury? I wondered. Maybe it was some bags of weed or something of importance to him. Whatever it was, I wanted to be quickly done with it. I went to the back of the car, opened the canopy and climbed in. I was surprised to see that another person was sitting at the back. I greeted him and he acknowledged and told me that his name was Yots. He was a young lad, in his late twenties or maybe a little older than that.

The car started moving. It moved slowly, weaving all over the road to avoid potholes. It turned into Ardbennie Road and followed this road until it turned into Maponga Road. From there, it turned into Mboto Street and then headed towards Simon Mazorodze Road. About a few hundred metres or so from the Radio Zimbabwe Studio, the car suddenly stopped beside the road. A man entered the car and sat in the front. The moment the gentleman got in, the car immediately began moving again, this time with more speed. Only when we were approaching the Mbudzi round-about did it slow down because of a traffic jam. It was now very dark outside. After navigating through the traffic jam, we continued on our journey. The car sped along the A4 highway for about twenty minutes or so. It then left the road altogether and drove into an adjacent small forest. After driving for a couple of minutes, the car finally stopped. We were now dead in the middle of the forest. I did not feel good about this, but I did not say anything. Yots handed me a pick and took one himself, while Maromo and the other guys grabbed the shovels.

"This is it," Maromo said, kneeling to the ground. "This is it. Let's dig here."

Yots immediately raised his pick and started digging. Not wanting to be outdone, I immediately followed suit. We did a pretty good job; within a few minutes, we had already dug up a sizeable hole.

"So, what are we going to bury here?" I asked as I continued to dig.

"Yots," Maromo called.

"Yes, boss."

"Do it."

As I was busy wondering what they could be talking about, something hit me on my head. All strength left my body, I immediately entered the world of oblivion.

"Hey boy! Hey! Wake up!" I could faintly hear someone calling me.

"Is he still breathing?" someone was asking.

"Yes, he is breathing." The man who was shaking me responded.

The dizziness was slowly starting to fade away, leaving in its place a throbbing pain. I was beginning to hear the voices more clearly now. I moved my hand and touched the top of my head. I shivered. It had now swollen into a large bloody bump.

"What's happening?" I mumbled to the man kneeling beside me.

"Calm down, don't strain yourself. I am a police officer, I am here to help you."

My pulse jumped when I heard him mention he was a police officer. With the haziness subsiding, I was becoming more and more aware of what was happening. I moved my hand around and realised that I was lying in the pit we had been digging earlier. Where were Maromo and the others? Why had Yots hit me on the head? I wondered.

"You are a very lucky young man. If we had been a few seconds late, you would have been dead. You are very lucky indeed."

"The others? Did you arrest them?" I asked.

"No. Unfortunately, we didn't. They all ran away. Don't worry too much about it though, we will catch them. I already know one of them. He's a colleague of mine," he said as he helped me to a sitting position. "Can you walk?" he asked.

I tried to get up but failed. My legs were still shaky. Seeing this, the two men eventually helped me to get out of the pit. They carried me to Maromo's car and helped me to get in. Maromo had apparently run away, leaving it behind.

"So what are we going to do?" the officer's companion asked.

"Go back to the kombi," the officer replied. "I will drive this one."

The officer immediately drove Maromo's car back to the city while being followed closely by his companion. Along the way, the officer told me that his name was Mutipitipi. He was a detective from the CID Homicide Department.

"How did you manage to find us?" I asked.

"Oh, it was pure luck, really. I just happened to be at the right place and at the right time. I had come to the funeral to talk to a certain friend of mine. That's when I saw this B2200. It had been mentioned by some guys who I had questioned earlier today. The moment I saw it, I immediately became suspicious and decided to follow it," he declared, visibly pleased with himself. Realising that I could now be dead if it weren't for him, I was happy for him myself. I owed the man the air I was breathing. So that pit I had helped to dig had been meant for me? How ironic, I had ardently dug a pit which had been intended to be my grave.

I turned and looked at him. "What's going to happen to me now?"

He shook his head, "I am sorry young man, it's now up to the courts. I don't know what may have made you mix with the wrong crowd but it's too late for you now. You must now face the law. If you tell the truth and display good behaviour, the judge may be a bit lenient on you."

With tears in my eyes, I nodded and remained quiet. I was now a prisoner, the drug ride had now ended, and there was no way around it. Detective Mutipitipi dropped me at Parirenyatwa Hospital, where I was immediately admitted. The doctor who examined me explained that the injury was not severe. By a quick of fate, I had not suffered any fracture from the knock I had received. After being discharged from the hospital, I was immediately sent to Harare Central Prison, a remand prison located on the eastern side of the city centre. I will have to admit that I was not at all prepared for what I saw there. When I was busy indulging myself with the drug money, I had not thought that I would end up there in my wildest dreams. They indeed do not build the castles of incarceration to be cosy. Life there is hard. The life there is brutal. After only a day of mixing with my fellow delinquents and dining in the insipid watery and undercooked meals, I was more than ready to talk. Detective Mutipitipi finally came on the third day to talk to me. I did not waste his time. I blurted out everything that I knew.

Detective Mutipitipi silently listened and jotted everything down.

"I am glad to tell you that we caught Maromo and all his accomplices," he said after I had finished my confession.

"All of them?"

"Yes," he said, smiling. "We conducted a manhunt yesterday. By the end of the day, we had managed to track all of them down. One of them has already confessed to being involved in the drug business and the murder in Zengeza. He also told us that Maromo is the one who shot the first victim who died in Mbare. Did you know about that?" I vigorously shook my head.

"No sir," I told him.

He nodded his head, believing what I had said. "There is, however, something important that I need to tell you Tichakunda."

"Something you need to tell me?"

"Yes."

"What is it?" I asked.

"Well, you see, what made the police extremely interested in catching these men was the fact that they had killed someone before. They killed the man five years ago in Mbare and had somehow managed to get away with it. They however made one terrible mistake. They used the same gun to kill again. That's how we managed to get them. But then, something very interesting happened. When I crosschecked John's records, I discovered that

John wasn't his real name. His real name was Mandikomborera Bungira."

"What?!" I jumped.

"I know, this shocked me too, but it's the truth. I just thought that I should let you know since you share the same family name. You're not related to the man, are you?"

"I am," I told him; tears starting to seep out of my eyes.

Detective Mutipitipi shook his head. "Well, this is so messed up."

It was indeed messed up. I was beginning to understand why Maromo had always looked at me with suspicion. It made sense now. I must have made him uncomfortable because I bore a close resemblance to my Uncle.

The detective told me to stay prepared since my trial was likely to begin soon. I spent the following two weeks holed up at the jail, waiting for my trial. During this time, I agreed to stand as a state witness in the case against Maromo and the others. This is where I learned the names of the other two guys. One was called Dean Kam, a businessman who owned an electronics shop located in the city centre. The other was, Tsunga, a police officer who had specialised in criminal drug cases.

Just before my trial, something happened which almost melted my heart. Nhengeni, mother Gombwe, Tindo and Natsai came to see me in prison. I was so happy and grateful to see them. They brought me some cooked food and a few books to read. I was particularly happy to see Natsai. I begged her to come and see me again, and she agreed. As she continued coming to see me, our friendship eventually grew into something more. She agreed to wait for me until I came out and even took care of my things which were about to be thrown away by my landlord.

My trial took place at the Harare Magistrate's Court. Since I had readily cooperated and agreed to stand as a witness in the trials of Maromo and the others, the magistrate was lenient. She slapped me with a four-year imprisonment sentence, two of which she suspended on a condition that I would not commit a similar offence in the future.

Tsunga received a 20-year sentence for his crimes, while Maromo, Yots and Kam received life sentences. They also named their boss, who was based in South Africa, which led to his arrest.

After my sentencing, I was sent here to Chikurubi maximum Prison where I am now. Natsai still visits regularly, and she is a pillar of my strength. As I now find myself with only three months of my sentence to go, I always think about my past mistakes. As some people say, we should not dwell on the past, but instead, we should try to focus on the future. That's a true statement, but as I have discovered, it's very difficult to forget the past. The mind cannot be erased like a flash drive. Some memories are eternal.

Although I can recall my past, all my experiences, whether good or bad, I always wonder how I got here. I feel as if I have been sleepwalking—a willing slumberer in a never-ending dream. Despite being a young man living in a deprived society, where there seems to be very limited choices, I could argue that I am a victim of ill-fated circumstances. But I don't know why, a part of me continuously shouts, reminding me that I could have done better. The other day, I was standing alone, gazing at the sky, when I suddenly remembered the conversation I had with that old man when I was younger, on the day I found my mother stabbed. I suddenly realised how profound his advice was. I still have a lot of unanswered questions, though. Maybe if he were here, he would have been able to answer some of them. I currently find myself at a point where each of us has passed at some stage in this capricious odyssey we call life. A stage where you sit and recall your past. That is where I am right now. I am reminiscing, reminiscing in the beyond.

Mmap Fiction Series

If you have enjoyed **In the beyond** consider these other fine books
in **Mmap Fiction and Drama Series** from *Mwanaka Media and
Publishing:*

The Water Cycle by Andrew Nyongesa
A Conversation…, A Contact by Tendai Rinos Mwanaka
A Dark Energy by Tendai Rinos Mwanaka
Keys in the River: New and Collected Stories by Tendai Rinos Mwanaka
How The Twins Grew Up/Makurire Akaita Mapatya by Milutin
Djurickovic and Tendai Rinos Mwanaka
White Man Walking by John Eppel
The Big Noise and Other Noises by Christopher Kudyahakudadirwe
Tiny Human Protection Agency by Megan Landman
Ashes by Ken Weene and Umar O. Abdul
Notes From A Modern Chimurenga: Collected Struggle Stories by Tendai
Rinos Mwanaka
Another Chance by Chinweike Ofodile
Pano Chalo/Frawn of the Great by Stephen Mpashi, translated by Austin
Kaluba
Kumafulatsi by Wonder Guchu
The Policeman Also Dies and Other Plays by Solomon A. Awuzie
Fragmented Lives by Imali J Abala

Printed in the United States
by Baker & Taylor Publisher Services